ICE
TIME

Books by David Skuy

Undergrounders

The Rocket series:
Rocket Blues
Last Shot
Ice Time

The Game Time series:
Off the Crossbar
Rebel Power Play
Making the Cut
Overtime
Double Shift

ICE TIME

David Skuy

Scholastic Canada Ltd.
Toronto New York London Auckland Sydney
Mexico City New Delhi Hong Kong Buenos Aires

Scholastic Canada Ltd.
604 King Street West, Toronto, Ontario M5V 1E1, Canada
Scholastic Inc.
557 Broadway, New York, NY 10012, USA
Scholastic Australia Pty Limited
PO Box 579, Gosford, NSW 2250, Australia
Scholastic New Zealand Limited
Private Bag 94407, Botany, Manukau 2163, New Zealand
Scholastic Children's Books
Euston House, 24 Eversholt Street, London NW1 1DB, UK

www.scholastic.ca

Library and Archives Canada Cataloguing in Publication
Skuy, David, 1963-, author
        Ice time / David Skuy.
Sequel to: Last shot.
Issued in print and electronic formats.
ISBN 978-1-4431-4893-1 (paperback).--ISBN 978-1-4431-4894-8
(html)
        I. Title.
PS8637.K72I24 2016   jC813'.6   C2016-901616-1
                                              C2016-901617-X

Cover photo © Igor Terekhov/Dreamstime.

6 5 4 3 2 1   Printed in Canada 139   16 17 18 19 20

To Mr. Hockey — as they say, he wasn't in a class all by himself, but it didn't take long to take attendance.
—D.S.

Special thanks to Baron Bedesky, Coordinator of Player Research and Relations, Professional Hockey Players' Association.

CHAPTER 1

The reporter shuffled over and held up her mic. "Check, check. Testing. Check, check. Is that good?"

The camera operator nodded. He held up three fingers and counted down. The red light on his camera turned on.

"Hi, Rita Martin for SportsInfo. I'm here with Bryan 'The Rocket' Rockwood, who's been turning some heads with his play at training camp. Bryan, what do you think of your chances of making the team?"

Rocket had done his share of interviews when he played junior hockey, but this was his first for the NHL. He cleared his throat nervously.

"The coaches are telling us rookies to approach it one day at a time. They said not to worry too much about the outcome. It's been awesome to play in a couple of exhibition games — great experience. Hopefully, I'm ready and I can help the team."

"So, Bryan — or do you prefer Rocket?" Martin said.

He smiled self-consciously. "Up to you, I guess. Most of the guys go with Rocket."

She laughed. "That's a better hockey name, I think.

Tell me, Rocket, what's the biggest adjustment you've had to make?"

"The game's a lot faster, for sure, and the guys are bigger. Your decisions have to be that much quicker, and you can never stop moving your feet. The intensity is very high: every shift, every drill."

"I know you've been asked about your size. Some people criticized management for spending a fifth-round pick on you because they said you're too small. You got cut from your minor bantam team because of that, right?"

This interview wasn't going the way he'd thought it would.

"I did, yeah — kind of an unpleasant memory. But the game's changing. It's all about speed and skill, so . . ."

"You spent two years in junior after getting drafted. Did that help?"

"I was disappointed to go back to junior, for sure. But we had an awesome season. The Axmen made the Memorial Cup, and Coach Alvo's the best. I learned a lot. I got invited to the junior national tryout, which was another great learning experience. Always tough to get cut, but the coaching staff wanted a . . . certain mix of players."

Cut because of his size — again. It was a huge blow that still stung.

But he forced a smile. "That's what hockey's about for me right now: keep learning, keep getting better."

"Thanks, Rocket," Martin said, "and good luck with the rest of camp." She faced the camera. "This is Rita Martin for SportsInfo, your source for sports. Back to you, Kevin."

The red light turned off.

"That was great," she said to Rocket. Then her head whirled to the right. "Oh, Jonathon, can I do a quick interview?"

She ran off, the camera operator trailing behind. Rocket had to laugh. Jonathon Daniels was the team's leading scorer last season, an all-star. Rocket was just a rookie trying to break in.

How long had he been dreaming of the NHL?

Forever.

How long had he been dealing with questions about his size?

Just as long.

The game had changed, though. Smaller guys were doing big things. He gave his head a shake and went back to the dressing room for his helmet and stick. Most of the guys were heading out for practice — big boys, mostly. This was a tough team that liked to play a physical style. Rocket had the bruises to prove it.

"Ready to roll, Rocket?"

Rocket looked up. "Hope so, Bossy."

"How was the interview?"

"Fine, until she asked why they'd drafted a shrimp like me." He laughed like it didn't really bother him.

Bossy snorted. "Ignore her. You know you belong."

That was easy for him to say. Bossy seemed even bigger than he had when they'd played together for the Axmen. Rocket was only five foot nine.

"I've been talking to a couple of the coaches," Bossy said, waving him closer. "They like what you're doing out there."

"All four centres are back from last year," Rocket

said. "I can't help obsessing on that. Those guys have one-way contracts. Why pay one of them a few million to play in the AHL when they can pay me the league minimum? It makes sense to send me down."

"It's a tough spot to be in."

"Whatever." Rocket gave Bossy's shin pads a whack with his stick. "Let's play hockey and let the coaches make the call. Bring it!"

Bossy grinned. "Always."

They punched gloves.

"See ya out there," Bossy said, heading for the ice.

Rocket pulled his helmet from his bag and put it on. A hand patted him on the back and he turned. "Coach Vic, how's it going?"

"All good. I wanted to let you know that we're holding a scrimmage to give the younger guys a chance. We want to see what you can do in a game environment." Vic was an assistant coach. He'd been good about helping the rookies transition to the pro game.

"Sounds great," Rocket said.

"We really want you to focus on both ends of the ice," Vic said. "We know your offensive game is good. That won't cut it, though. We need you solid in the defensive zone, too. When to go behind the net, when to support a defenceman — those decisions are critical. Don't try to do so much on offence that you leave us vulnerable to a counterattack."

He looked Rocket squarely in the eyes.

"I get it, Coach," Rocket said. "Forecheck, backcheck, paycheque."

Vic laughed and slapped the side of Rocket's

helmet. "Kids today — too much confidence. Now go out and do it."

Rocket got his stick and headed down the hall to the ice. Guys were skating around, stickhandling, taking shots, talking.

It was still hard to believe he was actually at an NHL training camp!

He was so close to making it. But clearly Vic had been giving him a message. He needed a strong scrimmage to answer questions about his defence. He'd been a high-scoring centre all his life. That reputation was hurting him. He took a few strides on the ice.

Forecheck, backcheck, and then maybe that paycheque would be his.

He turned on the jets, circling the net and powering up the side. He needed to burn off some nervous energy. He felt like he could skate through a brick wall.

So close.

CHAPTER 2

Jonathon Daniels chopped the back of Rocket's right leg with his stick. Rocket threw his elbow into Jonathon's chest and pushed off. He'd learned one thing at camp already — never back down.

Rocket's right winger was barrelling in on the fore-check, the puck in the corner. Rocket figured the opposing defenceman would probably try to shovel it up the wall to his winger. Decision time: Stay with Jonathon or trust his gut and head to the boards?

This was no time to play it safe. He had an NHL team to make. Rocket swerved and made a beeline to the boards. The defenceman reached out for the puck. Rocket grinned. He'd been right. The right winger lowered his shoulder. The puck was on the defenceman's stick for a fraction of a second — and then it went the opposite way behind the net to his partner camped out at the far post. The defencemen pressed up against the boards. Rocket's right winger hit him, but he absorbed the check easily.

Rocket felt sick. He'd left the middle of the ice wide open. He doubled back, but the defenceman snapped a pass to Daniels in the high slot, and just like that, it was a three-on-two the other way. Rocket could only lower his head and skate back hard. Daniels passed to his left winger, who bore down on Rocket's right defenceman. The opposing right winger on the far side drove for the net, which forced the left defenceman to go with him. That left Daniels open as the trailer. The pass came, tape-to-tape.

Rocket crossed the blue line, gathered himself and dove headlong, stick extended. His chest hit the ice hard. Daniels swung his stick, but all he hit was air. Rocket's desperation move had worked, and he'd knocked the puck to his right defenceman, who one-timed a pass to his right winger. Rocket hopped to his feet and charged back the other way.

The quick turnover caught the attacking side by surprise. Just like that, Rocket's line had the three-on-two.

Rocket took a pass in the neutral zone and distributed it quickly to his left winger, who cut into the middle of the ice. Rocket crossed behind him to take his spot on the left. The puck carrier gave it to the right winger, who carried it over the blue line, cut in and dropped it. The left winger picked the puck up, faked an inside move, and then went hard outside to the right.

Now it was Rocket's turn to be the trailer. He pushed on his inside edges and cruised into the high slot. The left winger sent a backhand pass his way. Rocket one-timed a snap shot, glove side, earmarked for the top corner . . .

Tweet!

The goalie flipped the puck to the referee. Awesome

save and he'd made it look routine. That would have been a sure goal in junior.

But this wasn't junior. It was tough to beat an NHL goalie without traffic in front. If they could see it, they could stop it.

"That's good for today, boys," Vic yelled from the bench. "Shower up, grab something to eat and we have a video session in room two."

Rocket curled across the ice to his bench to grab some pucks. He'd made a promise to himself to take two hundred shots a day.

"Hey, Bryan," Vic called. "Coach wants to talk to you."

Vic sounded serious. Rocket's heart began to beat a bit faster. He'd had a good scrimmage, and he'd almost got a goal on that last rush. Plus, he'd totally stopped Daniels on his three-on-two. He needed to play this cool, agree to anything: penalty killing, fourth line, even wing.

This was happening — for real.

He'd been working toward this moment since he put on his first pair of skates. It was his dream. And it wasn't about the money, though that would change everything, too. His mom was still struggling to make ends meet. Maddy was in her third year at university, and tuition and books were crazy expensive. They'd supported him for years; now it was his turn.

"Over here, Bryan," Vic said.

Coach Landry was waiting for him. Rocket took a deep breath and glided to the bench on one foot. He'd never really spoken to Coach Landry, other than a quick hi or goodbye.

"Good practice, Bryan," Landry said. "Have a seat on the bench."

Rocket wanted to remember every word of this conversation — the NHL!

"How'd you feel out there?" Landry said.

"Awesome, Coach."

Rocket wanted to kick himself. He sounded like a kid.

"Great, great," Landry said. "We wanted to have a quick word with you. I hope you've learned a lot at camp — and managed to have some fun. I know this is a business, but it's a game, too."

"For sure, Coach. The guys have been cool, lots of fun joking around in the room and stuff."

Of course, no one really talked to him except Bossy. This was a veteran team. They'd reached the conference finals last season. They weren't going to deal with a fifth-round-pick rookie.

"We've noticed you're a hard worker and a good listener," Landry continued. "That's very important, critical, in a young player's career. We all think you have potential."

Landry seemed to consider his next words carefully. "You're the classic case of a kid who's used to playing on the number-one line in minor hockey and in junior, but who maybe doesn't have the right size, tools or skill set to realistically be on the number-one line in the NHL — at least not for a while."

Rocket hadn't expected to knock Jonathon Daniels off the number-one line. No problem with that.

"That last play was an example," Vic cut in. "You gambled on the forecheck and gave Jonathon an easy breakout and a three-on-two."

"I knocked the puck away," Rocket said.

"We can't afford to give away high-quality chances like that," Vic said. "In a real game, with Daniels going a hundred percent, that could've been in the net."

"We project you as a number-three centre for the next few years: good on faceoffs, pop in the occasional goal and shut down opposing centres with your speed," Landry said. "That will take time because you're used to being a goal scorer first and a defensive centre second."

"We need to even that out," Vic added.

"This is all to say, we think it best that you go down to Pinewood and work on your two-way game, and then . . . and then we'll see," Landry said.

Rocket sat motionless. "I know I shouldn't have gone to the boards on the forecheck," he said finally, "and I definitely didn't get the shot off I wanted."

Landry grunted. "Go to the AHL, work hard, which I know you'll do, and become a first-rate, solid forward. And you can spend some more time in the weight room bulking up. Anderson McGill's a good coach. He'll teach you what it takes to make it in the NHL."

Landry stood up to leave. "Good luck and have a great season, Bryan. Vic will fill you in on what happens next. I have to prepare for the video session."

"Don't get too down," Vic said when Landry was gone. "It was close, but management wants to stick with the vets this year. They feel we can make a run for the cup. Besides, not many guys make the jump in their first camp."

"I know," Rocket managed. "I thought . . . I thought I was playing okay."

"This is a playoff team. Okay won't cut it," Vic said.

"Bossy made it as a rookie."

"He's six foot four and weighs two-hundred-and-fifty pounds," Vic said.

The response hit Rocket like a punch in the gut. The size issue never went away.

"The average size of an NHLer is six foot one and over two hundred pounds," Vic continued.

Like Rocket wasn't all too aware of that.

Vic seemed to realize it. "Listen, Bryan, things have a way of working themselves out. You'll see."

Rocket wasn't in the mood for a pep talk. "I'm good, Coach. Put my name down for the Frank J. Selke Trophy."

"Best defensive forward?" Vic laughed. "Good to set your goals high, I suppose."

Rocket stood up. "Thanks, Coach. For all your help."

Vic shook his hand. "Good luck, Bryan."

Rocket headed to the dressing room, mentally adding Vic and Landry to the list of people he would prove wrong.

Bossy met him at his stall. "So, it's Pinewood?" he asked quietly.

"Word gets around fast."

Bossy chuckled. "Hockey players are the worst gossips. Besides, we saw Landry talking to you on the bench. That's his signature move. Anyway, the AHL is good. You get paid, and you're an injury away from getting called up."

"They're saying my defence sucks," Rocket said.

"Landry's a defence-first kind of guy," Bossy said. "Stick with it. I'll see you back here soon enough, and then we'll get our line back together."

They bumped fists.

"Anyway. Let's get showered up, and I'll buy you lunch," Bossy said.

"Sounds good." But Rocket didn't think he could eat. He'd heard "too small" and "bulk up" before. But change his game? Guys spent years in the minors because they couldn't shake their reps for being bad defensive players.

Rocket bent down to untie his skates, then kicked them off angrily. He wasn't going to be one of those guys. He'd work so hard on his defence they'd have to take him back.

Frank J. Selke — the Rocket is coming for you. The thought almost made him grin.

CHAPTER 3

A gust of wind rushed into the café as Rocket opened the door. A few customers gave him irritated looks.

He'd found this place on a list: *Top Five Trendy Downtown Cafés*. It was in the heart of the theatre district. Supposedly, a lot of rich and famous people came here. If he had to tell his mom and Maddy he'd been sent down to the AHL, then he wanted to do it somewhere nice. They never went to places like this. He could only hope it wasn't *too* pricey.

He spotted an empty table and took a seat. A passing waiter looked him up and down and then moved on without a word.

The door opened. Again, those near the door scowled. Rocket waved. His mom and Maddy weaved through the tables. He gave them each a hug.

"Sorry we're late," his mom said. "The subway has become ridiculous. Delays every day."

"Risa and I waited at least fifteen minutes for a train," Maddy chimed in. She stuffed her backpack under the table and sat.

"Looks like you only have twenty kilos of books in

there," Rocket said to her. "Slacking off?"

"You slacked off at school enough for the both of us," Maddy said.

"Hey, I finished high school with the highest marks on my team," Rocket protested, "and I have two university credits."

"At that rate, you'll graduate when you're eighty," Maddy said.

A waiter stopped at their table. "Have you decided?" she said.

"Could you give us another minute, please?" Risa said.

The waiter looked around the restaurant. "It's kind of busy . . ."

"Sorry, but we just sat down," Risa said.

"We fill up quickly around lunchtime . . ."

"A coffee," Risa snapped.

"How do you want it?" the waiter said.

"In a cup."

The waiter went to another table.

Risa shook her head. "These snobby places are all the same. The waiters treat you like garbage if they don't think you're rich."

Maddy shook her head. Then she looked at Rocket. "So, *what's up?*"

That was Maddy for you — right to the point.

"Well, I got in late last night," Rocket said, "and I didn't want to wake you guys up. I went for a workout this morning, a bit early—"

"And you left a message to meet you here," Maddy interrupted. "So, what's up?"

"Yeah, okay. Get on with it, right?" He paused. "I

got sent down to the AHL, to a team called the Pine-wood Racers."

His mother's face fell. "Oh, Bryan, I'm so sorry. I know you were hoping for better news."

"I should be saying sorry to you," he said. "The money isn't bad. I've been offered a contract for around sixty grand a year. But . . . minimum contract in the NHL is over a half-million."

"Sixty thousand's still pretty good," Maddy said.

"But it's not NHL money," Rocket said.

"Where will you live?" his mother asked.

"I have to find a place. I'll have to pay for that, and for my own food."

"You'll be making a lot more money than you did in junior," Maddy jumped in. "You should be fine."

"But what about you guys? You'll be stuck in that crappy apartment. And how are you going to pay for med school, Maddy? I can help out, way more than I have been, but making the team would've solved everything." He slapped the table and shook his head. "I was so close. I could've paid your tuition and bought us a house."

His shoulders sagged, and he sat back in his seat, feeling overwhelmed. They all worked so hard, but there was never enough money. He'd really hoped to change that.

"The coaches are on me about my defensive-zone coverage," he said. "In the last scrimmage, I made a bad decision and went to the half-boards instead of . . ." He stopped, realizing it didn't matter. "Well, anyway, I'll be on a two-way contract in the AHL, so I still have a chance at making it. But that probably won't happen this year. If ever. I'm sorry, Mom."

"Honey, we'll be okay," she said, patting his hand.

"And you're not paying for my university," Maddy said. "I am."

"How are you going to do that?" Rocket said.

"My scholarship, plus grants and loans. I managed to save a fair bit from my job this summer, too."

"It's not enough," Rocket said. "We're a family, Maddy, and we help each other out. I know you're not technically my sister, but . . . you are, so get over it."

The waiter appeared. "Here's your coffee." She plunked it on the table. A bit spilled onto the saucer.

"Charming," said Risa.

"And here's your bill. There are people waiting for a table," she said before walking away.

Maddy glared after her, then turned back to Rocket. "Listen, you don't need to worry about me. The NHL is your *dream*, Bryan. You've worked your whole life for this, and you're going to make it. And not because we need the money but because you deserve to. You'll figure out the defensive-whatever, and you'll show them you're the real deal."

"That's right," said Risa. "You focus on what you need to do. We've always gotten by, and we always will."

"I'm still going to send you as much as I can," he said.

The waiter returned. "Are you going to pay for your coffee at some point?"

Risa reached into her purse, ripped open her wallet and slammed a five-dollar bill on the table. "I'll have my change, please."

The waiter rolled her eyes. "Thanks for the tip," she said as she walked to the cash register.

Rocket couldn't take it. He jumped up and marched over.

"Excuse me," he said.

The waiter arched her eyebrows.

"I want you to treat my mother with respect next time," he thundered.

"Why? Is she coming back to order another coffee, take up space and then leave a ten-cent tip?"

"Do your job."

"You're just three nobodies who came in to star-gaze," she huffed. "Your type bugs me. You want to be treated like you're famous, but you can't even afford to order something. A coffee? What a joke."

"I'll take the change," he growled.

She gave him the money. "Are you leaving?"

"We'll leave when we want." He stormed back. "Let's go."

"We haven't had a chance to talk to you," his mom said.

"That waiter is unbelievable. I hate it here. Everyone thinks they're so amazing because they have money. We'll come back when I'm in the NHL, and she'll be kissing my butt. You'll see. And I'll ask for the manager and get her fired."

"It doesn't matter," Risa said gently. "She's a rude person. No big deal. Let's go, then."

They had to walk by the waiter to get out. She smirked at Rocket, but he was too miserable to respond.

He'd let his mom and Maddy down.

His mom had made so many sacrifices for his hockey, spent so much money. She'd told him that as long as he wanted to play, she would make it happen — and she had.

Now it was time for him to make something happen.

CHAPTER 4

Somehow he'd walked right past the place. He was still fuming about that snooty waiter, and he hadn't been paying attention to where he was going. He doubled back and pushed on the door. It flew open and the handle hit the wall with a bang.

A waiter's head whirled toward the door. "You can just come in," he laughed.

"Sorry, just looking for some friends." Rocket scanned the restaurant.

"Yo, Rocket," André called out, waving his hand over his head. They'd found a table in the back corner.

Rocket went over. "Hey, guys, long time no see. How's school going?"

"It's barely started, and I'm already dreading my mechatronics class," Bird said.

"Mechatronics is an engineering course that combines several types of technology—" Megan began to explain to Rocket.

"Thanks, Ms. Education," he interrupted. It was hard to admit, even to himself, but Rocket felt dumb when he was with his non-hockey friends. Especially now that they were all in university.

Megan flushed deeply.

Rocket felt bad right away. He decided to change the topic.

"What else are you up to?" he asked Bird and Nigel.

Bird laughed and threw his hands in the air. "It's total mayhem. Nigel and I rented a place for this year, but it never occurred to us that it had no furniture. Are floors hard to sleep on?"

"I told you to start looking for stuff two months ago," Megan said.

"We kind of didn't take your good advice," Nigel said.

"Why do I bother?" she said.

"That's a solid question," Bird said with a grin.

Rocket had met Bird, Nigel and Megan when he was grade seven. Bird had always been chill and goofy. Nigel was usually very serious. And Megan was . . . Megan — in charge, smart and organized. He hadn't seen her much lately because of hockey. She was more like a woman than a girl now. She still wasn't into clothes or makeup, but she looked, well, more mature.

He'd met André in grade seven, too, when they'd played together for the Bowmont Blues. André had filled out even more over the years. He was probably two hundred pounds and well over six feet tall. Rocket felt a twinge of envy. That was NHL size. Of course, André had stopped playing hockey years ago.

"Forget about our boring lives," André said. "What's up with the Rocket? Your text said you're off to play for Pinewood."

Rocket told them what happened. "Now I have to become a different player — and fast," he finished.

"No problem," Bird said. "There's got to be a life-hack on that."

"I bet they tell rookies that all the time," André said. "Don't worry. They pay big bucks for guys who put the puck in the net."

"I thought I was so close, though," Rocket moaned. "I could literally taste that first contract."

"That's the problem," Megan said. "Guys get blinded by the money, and they forget their chances of making the NHL are tiny. I'm not being negative, Bryan, but this is why you should be taking those online courses. You can earn more university credits, and—"

"I can't," Rocket cut in. "The AHL is a pro league, with road trips and training. I have to focus on hockey."

"As opposed to before when you barely paid attention to it?" Megan said. "Hockey's all you ever do."

"Eat, sleep, play hockey — repeat." He grinned as André gave him a high-five.

"You can love the game," Megan said, "without risking your whole future. Think of all the guys who spent years trying to make it and had nothing to show for it when they didn't. You could be thirty years old, with no education and no job. And if you're seriously injured, then what?"

"Ya, keep your head up, bro," André said.

"And two hands on the stick," Nigel said.

"It ain't over till it's over," Bird added.

"That's more of a baseball saying, but it works," Rocket said.

"How about, it ain't over till the fat lady sings?" Bird asked.

"Never understood that one, but it's inspiring," Rocket said.

Megan rolled her eyes. "Very funny, gentlemen. But I'm serious, Bryan. I'm proud of you for finishing high school—"

"What choice did I have? You and Maddy would've killed me if I hadn't."

"Fair enough," Megan said. "I'm just saying, don't stop there. Get more university credits, get a degree, even if it takes a few extra years. Then, if hockey doesn't work out, you have a plan B."

"Is this your idea of a pep talk?" Rocket said.

"It's my idea of common sense."

Her eyes were fixed and hard, no trace of humour. None of the guys he'd played with put much effort into school. Most had done just enough to finish high school.

"Bird, Nigel, you're both in engineering, right?" Rocket said.

They nodded.

"You have four years of school to get your degree, and then you get a job."

"I might spend another year or two to get my master's and then look for a job, but that's about right," Nigel said.

"Okay, so however many years it is, how much is it costing you?" Rocket said.

"Don't ask," Bird said. "Tens of thousands."

"And what kind of money can you make?"

"I'm not sure," Nigel said. "First job might start at about fifty thousand."

Rocket looked triumphantly at Megan. "In one year in the NHL, I'll make more than they get in ten."

"That's if you make it," she said.

"You don't think I will?"

"I didn't say that."

"Because I'm too small?"

"Bryan, I—"

"My family needs this. I need this. I'm close. I know it," Rocket said. "Now's the time to work five times harder. I'll outwork the whole league, and when I get my next shot I won't blow it."

A few people at nearby tables looked over. He'd said that too loudly.

"Anyway, I should get going," Rocket said, standing up. "I'm leaving for Pinewood tomorrow morning. I'm lucky — I'm getting a lift with another guy on the team. I've barely seen my mom and Maddy, so . . . I'll have to catch up with you guys another time."

"Bryan, I didn't mean to . . . You just got here," Megan said.

"It's not that. Forget it. You guys have a great term at school, and we'll see each other . . ." He had no clue when he'd see them all again. They led such different lives.

"We can walk with you to the subway," Megan said.

"I know where it is," Rocket said.

Her face fell.

"I'm kidding. I . . . I got to run to a store or two and then get back to my mom's place. You guys may as well stay here."

An uncomfortable silence followed.

"I'll get out for a game once I figure out my schedule," André said.

"Awesome. Let me know when, and I'll score some tickets," Rocket said.

"Cool." André nodded.

"Take care, guys. Go engineering!" Rocket fist-bumped Nigel and Bird. "See ya, Megan."

She looked up. Her eyes were red. "Good luck," she said quietly.

"Thanks." Rocket looked around at his friends again. "Bye, guys."

He felt bad about Megan, but she just didn't get it. There was no plan B. It was the NHL or . . . He couldn't finish the thought. If he didn't make the NHL, then what else could he do? A feeling of dread spread in the pit of his stomach.

He was afraid. What would happen if Landry never trusted his defence? He could spend years in Pinewood, waiting for a call-up that never came. His speed and puck skills had always been the great equalizers, the reasons he'd beaten the odds despite being the smallest guy on the ice.

But speed and skill might not be enough this time.

CHAPTER 5

Rocket craned his neck. Still no car in sight. If this Rory Colbert guy blew him off, Rocket was in trouble. Only two buses went to Pinewood a day, one early in the morning and the other late at night. The first had already gone. The second wouldn't get there until after midnight, and he didn't have a place to stay.

"I really wish you had the name of a hotel," Risa said.

She'd been obsessing over where he'd stay since he got home yesterday.

"It's all organized," he said.

Very not true, but he didn't want his mom to worry. He was worried enough about just getting there. The Racers had a practice tomorrow morning at ten, and the general manager's email had made it clear they expected him to be on time.

Two vehicles approached. The first was a van, white and shiny and very new. The second was a small red old-model Toyota with a banged-up bumper. The van drove by. The Toyota pulled over. The window rolled down.

"Is there a Bryan Rockwood here?"

"That would be me."

Rory got out. He was a big guy, solid and thick, a touch under six feet. They shook hands. Rocket introduced his mom and Maddy, and Rory shook their hands, too.

"Thank you so much for giving Bryan a lift," Risa said.

"Not a problem. Lucky we're both going today. This came out of the blue for me. I've been working out all summer, and my agent's been calling and calling teams. Then Pinewood suddenly invited me out. I guess they've had a couple of injuries." Rory shrugged. "Part of the game, I guess. One guy's bad luck is another guy's opportunity."

"Have you played for this team before?" Risa asked.

Rory made a sour face. "Last team I played for was in the NHL, for three seasons. Then I blew my right knee out. That was two years ago. This is a bit of a comeback for me, I guess."

"Rory Colbert! I'm so dumb," Rocket said. "You played for the Rangers, right wing. I remember hearing you were out. How'd it happen?"

"It was kind of a nothing play. I came in on the forecheck, defenceman rang it around the wall, and I followed through on the hit." Rory shook his head. "Maybe I hit a rut or something, but I felt a burning in my knee. Next thing I know, I'm being carted off the ice."

"Brutal," Rocket said.

"Yep." Rory nodded. "Anyway, I guess we should get going."

Risa teared up.

"Pinewood's only a couple hours away," Rocket said softly. He gave her a hug.

"Me, too," Maddy said. They hugged.

"Life of a hockey player," Rory said. "Always on the move. My wife hates it."

"It must be hard on her," Risa said.

"She's tough."

"Where'd you meet?" Maddy asked.

"Maddy, we have to go!" Rocket said.

Rory laughed. "It's okay. Melissa and I actually started going out in grade nine. Crazy, eh? We have a little girl now, Angela. She's eleven months."

"Oh my gosh, still a baby," Risa said. "Melissa will have her hands full. They're not coming to Pinewood?"

"We'll see. Her parents are here in town, and so are her friends. She'd be alone in Pinewood, and with road trips and stuff, we figured she should stay here until things are more settled."

"Any pictures of Angela?" asked Maddy.

Rory pulled out his phone.

"So cute," Maddy gushed.

"She's adorable," Risa said. "I assume that's mommy." She pointed at the woman in the photo.

"That's my Melissa."

Rocket snuck a look. Angela was pretty cute. In the picture, she sat happily perched on Melissa's knees.

He turned to Rory, "Should I put my stuff in the trunk?"

"It's packed with my stuff," Rory said. "Toss it in the back seat."

Rocket picked up his hockey bag and sticks and grabbed his suitcase with his other hand.

"This is really nice of you, Rory," Risa said. "And it's great that Bryan will know someone on the team before he starts."

Rocket opened the car door and put his stuff in.

"Takes me back," Rory said. "I spent two seasons in the AHL, too." His face darkened. "Hopefully, I'll move up sooner this time." He took his keys out of his pocket and got in the car. "It was nice to meet you both," he said through the window.

Rocket opened the passenger door. "I'll text you when I get there," he said to his mom and Maddy.

He got in and waved. Then Rory turned the car on and they drove off. Rocket could see his family in the side mirror, still waving.

"Sorry about all the questions," Rocket said.

"No problem. Coaches talk about the team being a family. It's not true. I learned that the hard way. Your mom and Maddy? They're your family. They'll be there for you long after hockey is done. The NHL is a business, and we're nothing but pieces of meat. You can't play, you get tossed in the garbage. That's just the way it is."

Rocket didn't know what to say.

"I never would've made it back to this point without my family supporting me," Rory said. "I know this is my last shot, though. I've been out too long."

Rocket thought about Megan. "I guess hockey has to end sometime."

"All I've ever done is play," Rory said. "I thought I'd have at least ten years in the NHL. Now look at me, a gimpy knee and a wife and a baby. This wasn't the plan."

"Your knee's probably stronger than before, with all the working out."

"Take care of your body," Rory said. "That's the best advice I can give. Don't let anyone force you to take chances with your health. I'd hurt the knee a few games before, but the training staff convinced me it would be fine. Turned out I had stretched some ligaments, which weakened the knee. I was in the final year of my contract, too. They put me on waivers when they knew how serious it was. No one picked me up, so basically, I'm a free agent."

Rory paused and then laughed. "Hey, bro, sorry for all this wailing about poor me. It's still hockey. We'll have some fun on the ice and kick some butt. And it'll be cool to be back in the room with the boys. I love Angela, but I'm not going to miss changing diapers."

Rocket laughed, happy to lighten the mood.

Rory shifted in his seat and winced. "Do you drive, by any chance?"

"Sorry. We don't have a car. I never got my licence."

"No big deal. Just hoped you could drive at some point. My knee's bugging me. Whatever. You want to listen to some tunes?"

"Sure."

"What're you into?"

"Whatever you like."

Rory took out his phone. "Let's go with some old-school R&B to set the tone, then we'll drift into some house and electronica. Cool?"

"Sounds good."

Rory turned up the volume.

Rocket looked out the window. His nerves kicked up. Rory's story had shaken him. One injury and it could be all over.

CHAPTER 6

Rocket was almost disappointed when they pulled up in front of the Pinewood Barns Arena. Rory was a great guy, and they'd ended up talking a lot more than listening to music.

It turned out Rory was just as nervous as Rocket — and just as eager to catch the big club's attention. They both wanted to play hard and move up.

"You sure this is where they told you to go?" Rory said.

They hadn't told Rocket anything, but he didn't want to hold Rory up. It was nice enough that he'd given him a ride. Rocket grabbed the handles of his hockey bag and suitcase.

"I'm good. See you at tomorrow's practice. And thanks again," Rocket said.

After Rory left, Rocket rolled his bags into the arena lobby. A man and a woman were chatting by the ticket booth, their heads close together.

"Excuse me, do you know where I'd find the Pinewood Racers' office?" Rocket said.

The man pointed to a set of stairs. "Up there."

"Are you with the team?" Rocket said.

"I'm the arena manager," the man said. "We're with Floyd Entertainment."

"Do you mind if I leave my stuff here? I have to speak to someone in the office."

The man shrugged and turned back to the woman.

"Tell the staff to come early tomorrow," he said to her. "Floyd wants the offices cleaned."

"We just did them."

"Floyd said the dust bothers Queen Stella."

Rocket climbed the stairs as he listened to them. He'd done some online research about the Racers. The Floyd family had owned the team for something like forty years. Raymond Floyd was the president and executive general manager. Kirk Blywood was the general manager. Rocket had no idea about this Queen Stella.

Upstairs, a woman was vigorously mopping the hallway. Rocket knocked on Blywood's office door.

"No one is in," the woman said.

"Thanks," Rocket told her. He texted Blywood. He didn't hold out much hope for a response, since the guy hadn't returned any of his texts today.

He should have listened to his mom. Stupid to just show up. Blywood could be anywhere.

Rocket went back down to the lobby. The man and the woman were gone.

"Thanks for watching my stuff," he muttered.

He sighed and rolled his neck, then googled *hotels in pinewood*.

Hotels were expensive. He tapped on the cheapest, which was eighty-nine dollars a night. There was no way he could afford to stay there for more than a day or two. He'd have to catch Blywood before practice in the morning to ask for some recommendations.

Rocket wheeled his stuff over to the main street to hail a cab. He had no idea where the hotel was. It hadn't looked far on the map, but it was hard to tell.

He waited and waited, but no cabs went by. Finally, after ten irritating minutes, he searched for a company on his phone, filled out a request form and sent it in.

Using his hockey bag for a seat, Rocket scrolled through the Pinewood Racers' website to pass the time. Their leading scorer was Cam Conner, and he looked like a serious player. He'd been in the AHL for almost ten seasons and had been an all-star a bunch of times. Over the years, he'd also played some games in the NHL.

A car pulled up. "You call a cab?"

"Yeah."

"I've been waiting at the rink."

"I wrote that I was on the street."

"You said the rink. Why not wait at the front door?"

"Because I was already on the street."

"You should've been where you said you'd be. You wasted my time."

"I am where I said I'd be!"

"Forget it."

The taxi drove off.

"Thanks, jerk!" Rocket yelled. He grabbed his sticks and gave his hockey bag a whack. Then he called the cab company.

"Sunnyside Taxi, what's the address?"

"I called a cab and he drove off on me," Rocket said.

"What's your phone number?"

He told her.

"You weren't waiting at the rink," she said.

"I filled out the form . . ." He groaned. "Can I get another one?"

"Where are you?"

"Exactly where I said I was!"

The line went dead.

Rocket closed his eyes. So far life as a pro player sucked.

He waved at a cab as it raced by, but it had people in it. Behind it was a small Honda Civic. It stopped. There were four boys inside.

"Yo, bro, where're you going?" a kid asked, leaning out the passenger-side window.

He looked like a high-school student.

"I'm going to a hotel. Not sure of the address. Hold on," Rocket said. He checked his phone. "Do you know where Lakewood Avenue is?"

"This is Lakewood," the kid said.

"Do you know the Lakewood Hotel?" Rocket said.

The boys laughed.

"It's just down the street — that white building," the kid said.

Rocket looked in dismay. Now he saw it: *The Lakewood*. The sign wasn't big, but still, he should have checked the map closer.

"I guess I'm a bit disoriented. I'm new in town," he said, picking up his hockey bag and sticks.

The rear window opened. "Who do you play for?" a voice called out.

"The Pinewood Racers."

The car exploded in cheers.

"Awesome, bro. What's your name?" the kid in the front said.

"Bryan . . . Rockwood."

Behind the driver, in the back seat, a boy shook a yellow-and-black scarf out his window. The wind caught hold, and it stretched out — *Pinewood Racers.*

Rocket grinned. "Go, Racers!"

"I'm Crawford," the kid in front said. "This is Rino driving."

Rino honked the horn.

"Chaz is behind me," Crawford went on, "and Griff has the scarf. He loves that thing."

"Nice to meet you guys," Rocket said.

"I think I've heard of you," Crawford said. "You played for the Axmen."

"Guilty," Rocket said.

"We'll see you at the opener on Saturday," Crawford said.

"What number are you?" Chaz asked.

The boys reminded Rocket of someone — himself. Hockey obsessed.

"Not sure about the number, or the game. We'll see. Tomorrow is my first practice," Rocket said.

Rino honked the horn a few more times.

"Good luck!" Crawford said.

The boys began to chant, *"Go, Pinewood, go! Go, Pinewood, go!"* as the car pulled away, Griff's scarf flapping madly in its wake.

Rocket crossed the street and walked down to the hotel. After checking in, he flopped on the bed as soon as he got in the room. He was tired. The past few days had been a blur — sent down by Landry, telling his family, meeting his friends, getting ready to go, the drive up, trying to find a place to stay.

He texted his mom and Maddy, so they wouldn't worry: *Everything is great. Psyched for practice tomorrow. Speak soon.*

He texted Megan: *Good 2 see U yesterday. All's fine here. About 2 look up some courses and see what's available.*

Then he tossed his phone aside and turned on his laptop. He typed *Pinewood Racers* into the YouTube search bar. Videos from last year popped up. The first was called *C.C. Storms the Ice*. It was about Cam Conner, so C.C. had to be his nickname.

Rocket clicked on the video. He'd look up online courses later.

CHAPTER 7

The dressing-room door opened. In walked a large man with wavy blond hair, a square jaw, long, thick arms and massive thighs — the absolute picture of a pro hockey player. He shook hands with a bunch of the guys. Rocket knew him from the website — Cam "C.C." Conner.

"R.C. Cola," C.C. said as he greeted Rory. A huge grin was plastered across his face. The two men embraced.

Rocket laughed to himself. Rory Colbert — R.C. Cola — a good hockey nickname.

"Bro, I was so psyched when I heard you were here. How's the knee?" C.C. said.

Rory bent his right knee and stomped the floor. "Good enough to smoke you on the outside."

"I don't doubt it," C.C. roared, and they high-fived. "Goldsy, come say hi to a real hockey player."

"Nice to finally meet one," Goldsy said.

Rocket recognized him, too — Ben Goldsworthy, left winger. He'd played on C.C.'s line last season.

"Meet another player," Rory said, nodding at

Rocket. "This is Bryan Rockwood. I think people call him Rocket."

C.C. and Goldsy shook Rocket's hand.

"Have you spoken to Coach Mack yet?" C.C. asked Rory.

"Nah. Got the lowdown from Blywood this morning, though," Rory said.

Rocket wondered how. Blywood still hadn't returned any of his texts about places to stay. And he hadn't been around when Rocket got to the arena early that morning. Instead, Rocket ended up talking to the trainer, Nadav, who told him guys find their own places — not what Rocket wanted to hear.

Before practice, Rocket had found a few places online and booked some appointments for that afternoon.

A man walked into the dressing room, and Rocket did a doubletake. It couldn't be. Their eyes met.

"The Rocket's in the AHL? Seriously?" The man chuckled and looked around as if he couldn't believe it. "I cut this kid in minor bantam, no kidding. I was coaching a AAA team. Takes me back a few years."

C.C. looked uncomfortable. "Coach Barker, this is Rory Colbert," he said, changing the subject.

"The one and only R.C. Cola. Awesome to have you," Barker said. "I'm new to the Racers, too. I'm here to get this crew to play some defence. The Racers are going to be about puck possession this year. We'll be a NHL-style team, so it's cool to have a real NHLer."

"Looking forward to being back on the ice," Rory said.

Barker looked over at Rocket. "By the way, this isn't

junior, Rockwood. I'll be introducing you to your own end."

"We've met," Rocket said, as sarcastically as he could.

Barker grunted and his eyes narrowed. "We're on the ice in fifteen minutes." He clapped his hands a few times. "Let's get going."

C.C. and Goldsy went to their stalls to get dressed. Rocket pretended he had to retie his skates so he could hide his rage.

This was bad in so many ways. Sure Barker had cut Rocket, but then he'd asked him to come back. Rocket had refused, and Barker had hated him ever since. Things hadn't improved when they'd both moved up to junior — every time their teams met it was nasty.

"Don't worry about that guy," Rory said quietly. "First-year coaches always act tough. They want to establish a rep. He's no big deal."

"We have a bit of a history," Rocket said.

Rory slapped Rocket's shin pads. "We both have to turn the page and start fresh."

Nadav came in. "Ice is ready if you want to get out there," he said.

Rocket reached for his sweater. He'd been number 18 since he was a kid, but it was gone. Instead, he'd chosen number 36 — he'd be twice the player he used to be. He put it on, grabbed his stick from the rack and headed out.

The moment his skates cut into the glistening ice, his problems seemed to disappear. Hockey was like that. Life was the hard part.

He skated leisurely around the net. A few more guys

came out. Barker was stacking piles of pucks on the boards by the bench. Rocket veered off to get one.

"Can you lift the puck off the ice yet?" Barker chirped.

Rocket stickhandled in on goal, reared back and blasted a slapshot into the top right corner, just under the crossbar.

"Chew on that, Bark-Breath," he said.

His friend Adam had come up with that name for Barker way back — during their tryouts for that bantam team. Wait until Adam and their friend Ty heard Barker was in the AHL.

It had been a while since Rocket had talked to Adam and Ty. All three of them had made it to junior, but only Rocket was still playing. Ty had been a high first-round draft choice and played three years. He'd hurt his knee, though, and after surgery, he decided to quit. He was in university now, apparently thinking about law school. Adam had quit after two seasons — said he wasn't into it. He was at university, too, but he didn't take his studies that seriously. He was more into having fun.

Ty and Adam didn't have to worry about the future. Their families were rich.

A short, pale man came onto the ice. His thin jet-black hair was brushed straight back, as if every hair had been glued in place. His eyes were close together, but big, almost too large for his face. He was looking all over the ice, first the stands, then the benches and then behind both nets. He skated slowly, maybe even a bit awkwardly. A whistle hung from a string around his neck.

On second glance, Rocket realized the man was

Anderson McGill, the Racers' head coach. McGill wasn't a typical coach because he'd never played hockey at a high level, not even junior. He'd started out coaching minor hockey, then community college and university, before landing the Pinewood job last year.

McGill stopped at centre, and the guys formed a semicircle in front of him.

"No point talking about that last exhibition game," he said. "Effort level wasn't bad, but we didn't have the puck enough. We lost way too many draws. We can't control the puck if we give away possession so much."

"We lost fifty-seven percent of the draws in our end," Barker piped in, "and sixty-two percent in theirs."

McGill looked tired. "We're going to correct that. Anyway, I believe we have a couple of new guys . . . Coach Kaufman?"

Rocket hadn't seen Kaufman yet. He was the special teams coach. With his broad chest, thick legs and big forearms, he looked more like a hockey player. He wore a Racers baseball cap and sweatshirt.

"Thanks, Coach Mack," Kaufman said. "Everyone say hello to Rory 'R.C. Cola' Colbert."

The guys banged their sticks on the ice.

"Hi, boys. Good to be here. Hope we have a great season," Rory said.

"And . . ." Kaufman paused to look at his clipboard. "Bryan Rockwood. Where are you?"

"Right here," Rocket said.

Kaufman nodded. "Hi, Bryan. You're a centre, right? Hopefully, you'll help with the faceoffs."

"We'll see about that," Barker quipped.

A few guys laughed. One player to Rocket's right, number 22, didn't look too amused.

"C.C., get everyone down to one end," McGill said.

"You got it, Coach Mack. Let's move it, boys," C.C. said.

He skated off to the far net, the guys following behind. Rocket felt a stick slap his shin pads.

"Time to bring it," Rory said. "C.C. filled me in. Management is looking to make changes. Floyd — the owner — is insane. He wants a championship this season, and McGill is under serious pressure to produce. Floyd's not happy with their first-round loss in the playoffs last season, and the Racers only won two exhibition games this year. That's why Floyd replaced the defence coach with that Barker guy."

"Okay, so we'll both bring it," Rocket said, slapping Rory's pads.

It was weird that Rory said "bring it." That's what Rocket, Ty and Adam used to say to psych each other up.

And "changes"?

Well, Rocket was going to be on the roster when the dust settled.

He had to be.

CHAPTER 8

Barker tapped his stick on the ice. "Strauss, take offensive centre. R.C. Cola, take right wing for the defending side. Guys, watch how a pro plays — hard every shift."

Strauss was number 22. Rocket had thought he was a winger. The website said he was.

"Straussy, all yours," Goldsy said. He was the offensive left winger for the drill.

Strauss approached the dot to the goalie's left.

Rocket rolled his shoulders. His muscles were tight. He'd been watching them practise faceoffs and breakouts for twenty minutes now — just ten guys fighting for possession of the puck until the defensive team got it over the blue line. So dull.

Kaufman was running the drill, but Barker kept chirping away, especially at whoever lost a draw. Never to C.C., though. McGill watched in silence, his eyes moving constantly, like he was expecting a sneak attack.

Strauss lost three draws in a row — cleanly. Rocket could tell he wasn't used to taking faceoffs. Barker looked disgusted.

In junior, Rocket had consistently won over sixty

percent of his draws. If the Racers needed faceoff help, this could be his ticket into the starting lineup.

Kaufman looked his way. "Rockwood, come take a draw for the defence."

C.C. backed away. "Have fun, boys," he said. He tapped Strauss's shin pads, and then gave Rocket's a slap as he skated to the bench.

Desperate to make a good first impression, Rocket's mind whirled. The faceoff was to the goalie's left. Strauss liked to bend low, his hands way down on the shaft, legs spread far apart. Rocket knew exactly what to do. Strauss would be quick, but he'd have no power.

Rocket fixed his gaze on the puck.

It dropped. But Rocket ignored it and blocked Strauss's stick. The puck bounced. Rocket lowered his right shoulder and pivoted on his right skate, and in one motion, he swept the puck back to the corner. Strauss was caught off guard, and he dropped to one knee. This meant Rocket didn't have to block him out to prevent a forecheck.

The left defenceman snapped a short pass behind the net to his partner, who took a few backwards strides to clear the net and draw Goldsy to him. Then he saucered a pass to Rory, who had hustled over to the right wall. Rocket curled in front, headed up-ice and took a sharp pass from Rory a metre below the top of the circle. The defencemen had long since given up the blue line, having no choice once Rocket had won the draw so cleanly. The breakout was basically unopposed.

The whistle sounded, and Rocket backhanded the puck behind him and continued across to the bench. That felt good.

A defenceman threw an elbow into Rocket's shoulder as he skated by. Rocket spun and fell to the ice.

"Didn't they teach you to keep your head up in junior?" the defenceman said. He skated off.

"Get up, Rockwood. You can have a nap later," Barker yelled. "Get back for another draw."

Rocket growled under his breath. But rookies had to earn respect. He got that.

Strauss lined up exactly as before. It looked like he was gripping his stick tightly, and his eyes were blazing. Rocket knew that look — too stressed, too uptight. Strauss wanted to win the draw too badly.

Kaufman held the puck out. Strauss went early and swung his stick. Kaufman pulled the puck back. Technically, Strauss should be out of the circle. Rocket stood up and rolled his shoulders back.

"Put your stick down, Rockwood. Geez. Hurry up," Barker said.

Rocket ignored him and set up. The puck dropped. Rocket drove his top hand forward and pulled back on his left hand, which was lower. His blade nicked the puck and sent it back between his feet, and in the same motion, he spun into Strauss to block him from pressuring the puck carrier.

Rory did a nice job boxing Goldsy out, so the defenceman Rocket had passed to had nothing but open ice. He rounded the net and gave Rocket a soft pass. Again, the opposing defencemen had to give up the blue line. Rocket crossed the line and then snapped a very hard pass to the defender who'd elbowed him — just to give him something to think about. He curled back to the defensive zone to set up against Strauss again.

Rocket didn't know much about Strauss as a player, but it was tough to move from wing to centre if you weren't used to taking draws. Still, he needed to work on his faceoffs.

McGill pulled on Kaufman's sleeve and said something to him.

"Straussy, take a seat," Kaufman said. "C.C., take his spot."

Strauss hung his head and skated slowly to the bench. A few guys tapped his shin pads.

Rocket bent over, stick across his knees. Huge test. C.C. was very skilled. He hadn't lost many draws. He was a right-handed shot, and he favoured the reverse grip.

The draw was still to the goalie's left, which meant C.C. would be trying to send the puck to his right defenceman near the boards. Rocket looked over to Rory and ever-so-slightly nodded at the faceoff dot. Rory nodded back.

Rocket was loving Rory. He totally understood: Rocket would tie C.C. up, and Rory would come over and take the puck.

Barker held the puck over the dot. For some reason he'd taken over from Kaufman.

"Set up, already," he said to Rocket.

"I'm coming," Rocket said.

Barker just dropped the puck. C.C. whisked it back to the right point.

"What was that?" Rocket said.

Rory and Goldsy straightened up. They assumed Barker would call it back.

He didn't.

The puck went to the left defenceman. C.C. slipped

past Rocket as the defenceman let the puck go. The goalie stopped it with his right pad, but the puck dropped in front. C.C. grabbed the rebound, cut left with the puck on his backhand and flipped it high into the net over the goalie's arm.

"How was that a faceoff?" Rocket said to Barker.

Barker jabbed him in the chest with a finger. "You cost your team a goal. Pros don't give up on a play. Ever. You'd better figure that out real quick, or it'll be the East Coast League for you — which is probably where you belong." He turned away. "C.C., nice hands in front."

Rocket was too angry to talk. He gripped his stick tightly, shifted his weight back and forth on his skates and set up for the draw. Ridiculous.

"Take a seat, Rockwood," Barker said. "Watch how the professionals play. Beauclair, take defensive centre."

Rocket popped his mouthguard out and skated off. No one said a word to him. He reached behind the boards for some water, tilted his head back and took a long sip.

Suddenly, he got the feeling he was being watched. He lowered the bottle and looked across the ice. McGill and Kaufman were looking right at him. Kaufman turned and began talking to McGill. The head coach merely nodded, his face cold and hard. Rocket lowered his gaze.

Barker dropped the puck. C.C. knocked it to the wall.

Rocket put the water down and pressed his back against the boards.

"Bring it, Rockwood," he whispered to himself.

CHAPTER 9

Nadav was coming out of the dressing room, and he held the door for Rocket, who was coming in.

"Getting in a little extra skate?" Nadav said.

Rocket had stayed out after practice to take some shots. He shrugged. "I watched most of the practice. Needed to work off some energy."

Nadav smiled warmly. "I was watching. You can really move out there. They call you Rocket, right?"

"That's more to do with my last name — Rockwood."

Nadav chuckled. "Maybe."

Rocket was embarrassed to admit the real reason he'd stayed out — to show off his skills. Hopefully, one of the coaches had been watching.

He would work hard on his defensive game. He'd commit to that. But like André said, NHL teams paid the big bucks for goal scorers, and that's what Rocket was.

Looking at the clock, he saw he was pushing it. He'd agreed to meet someone in an hour to see an apartment. It didn't look like the nicest place, but it was close to the rink. He had three other places to see after that one. He sat and began untying his skates. The guys were joking around, the usual dressing-room banter.

This was hardly Rocket's first new team. He knew the drill. Keep quiet and be cool. Prove yourself on the ice first, and then the guys would accept you. Rory was talking with C.C. and Goldsy. Rory didn't have to prove himself. He'd played more games in the NHL than anyone in this room.

C.C. showed Goldsy his phone. "Yeah, that's right. I'll be golfing with Ray-Ray in an hour."

Goldsy gave C.C. a shove. "So what? You carrying his bag?"

"It'll be golf carts all the way," C.C. said. "You know Ray-Ray. He's too lazy to walk the course."

Rocket wondered who Ray-Ray was. C.C. didn't seem to think much of him.

"R.C. Cola, you golfing much these days? I could see if Floyd needs someone," C.C. said.

Floyd was the owner. Did the guys call him Ray-Ray?

"Thanks, bro, but I'll take a pass," Rory said. "I haven't played in a couple of seasons. I'm going to hit the bike and then stretch." He unstrapped his knee brace.

Nadav came back in, cleared this throat and nodded at Strauss. "Floyd wants to talk to you, Straussy. In Blywood's office."

"My wife's waiting for me in the stands," Strauss said. "Can we talk tomorrow before the game? I'll come in early."

Nadav's eyes softened. He looked sad. "They want to do it now. Sorry."

The room quieted down. Rocket felt bad for Strauss. He didn't know the guy, but he had a feeling he was in for a serious lecture about faceoffs. His wife would have to wait a little longer.

"Tell them . . . tell them, I'll be there in a minute," Strauss said.

"Sure, Straussy. No problem." Nadav backed up to the door. "Guys, don't forget to leave your stuff out to dry," he said to rest of the team. "We'll run the fans today."

"You'll never get the stink out of Goldsy's equipment," C.C. said. "He gets pretty nervous in the corners."

"I might not shower, I smell so good," Goldsy said. He struck a body-builder pose.

C.C. threw a towel at him.

"Listen up, boys," C.C. said when Nadav had gone. "Ray-Ray will be speaking to us before the game tomorrow, so get here a little early and watch the language. He'll be bringing Queen Stella, too. Apparently, she's our good-luck charm."

"Please don't tell me she's singing the anthem," Goldsy said.

"It's opening night," C.C. said with a grin.

Goldsy towelled the sweat from his head. "I need a daddy like Floyd's. All my dad ever bought me was some hockey sticks. Floyd gets an AHL team."

"Speaking of money, Ray-Ray better be in a generous mood and feed me this afternoon," C.C. said. "There has to be some perk to hanging out with him."

He headed toward the showers, but stopped in front of Strauss. "I'll give you a call later," he said quietly.

Strauss nodded, then got up and shook hands with a few guys. After he left, they leaned their heads together and began to whisper.

"Floyd must be a fearsome guy," Rocket said to Rory. "Strauss looks like he's seen a ghost."

"At this point, Strauss would probably rather see a ghost," Rory said. "Hey, what's the deal with you and Barker?"

Rocket told him about Barker taking over his minor bantam team, then about his run-in with Barker at the junior draft. Finally, he talked about how they'd gotten into it during the games that followed.

"You should probably fix that," Rory said. "Barker strikes me as a guy who's full of himself. Butter him up by asking him to explain something — the simpler, the better. Gives him a chance to sound like a hockey genius, and it'll make him think you're in awe. Do it a few times, and he should get off your back. He totally hosed you on that faceoff, by the way, so don't worry about it." He headed off to shower.

Rocket stacked his equipment to dry. He and Barker seemed to be connected in some strange way. They kept running into each other. Hockey was a fairly small world, so maybe it wasn't that weird. But couldn't the guy let go of something that had happened ages ago? Rocket had only been twelve!

Rory was right. Rocket would butter Barker up and ask for advice. The "suck up" was the perfect play.

He felt better already. Hopefully, the apartment would be okay, and he'd get that out of the way. Then tomorrow he'd have the best game of his life.

CHAPTER 10

Rocket choked back a cough as the bus pulled away, leaving a belch of black smoke. That trip took a lot longer than he'd thought — forty minutes. He should have checked the distance to the arena. There'd be a lot of travel time if he lived here.

The first three places he'd looked at were near the arena, but they were crazy expensive. Plus, they weren't furnished, so he'd have to spend a fortune on furniture and kitchen stuff.

This was the last viewing he'd booked. If this didn't pan out, he'd have to stay in the hotel even longer. At this rate, he wouldn't have anything left to send home for Maddy's tuition.

He looked around. This place reminded him of his old neighbourhood, and that wasn't a good memory. The buildings were old and grey, the stores generally rundown and small — ma-and-pa shops, or fast food. He noticed a dingy second-hand clothing store and a lot of bars.

He checked the address on his phone. This was definitely it — 78 Headley Avenue. It was a squat, ugly red-brick apartment building with small balconies running up each side of the front. A few units had air conditioners sticking out of windows. Rocket pressed the superintendent button.

"Hello?" a man said.

"Hi . . . It's Bryan Rockwood. I emailed you about the place for rent."

"Who is it?" Rocket heard a woman ask.

"Someone is here to see the room," the man said.

The door buzzed, and Rocket went into the lobby.

The room? How small was the apartment?

To his right, he noticed a door with a gold nameplate: *Superintendent*. The door opened, and a short, slight man with thick black hair and a big smile stepped out. His eyes were bright, his movements quick and decisive, and his handshake was firm. Rocket took an instant liking to him.

"Very nice to meet you, Bryan. I am Ricardo, but everyone calls me Ritchie, ever since I was a little boy. I am thirty-six years old, and still I am called by my boy name." He laughed heartily and motioned Rocket to come into his apartment.

"That's kind of a coincidence — you're thirty-six and that's my new hockey number," Rocket said.

Ritchie's eyes grew big. "You are a hockey player? I was thinking you are here for schooling. We get many students in this place. But who do you play with?" His English wasn't the best, and he had a heavy accent. Rocket wondered where he came from.

"I'm playing for the Pinewood Racers, the AHL team."

"My son loves hockey very much. I do not understand it well, but I like it, too. We play mostly football where I come from — what you call soccer." He paused. "The Racers play hockey at the Pinewood Barns, yes?"

"That's right."

"My wife is working there, as a cleaner." Ritchie's smile faded. "They do not treat her very nice. But it gives more pay than fast food places." Suddenly, his good humour seemed to return, and he laughed. "We knew we would be making much sacrifices to come here, but our children will have a better life. So we will work hard. Anyway, please come in and see the room."

But instead of leading Rocket to another apartment, he pointed into his own unit.

"The room is where exactly?" Rocket said.

"Rafa and Leona will move in together, and you can take Rafa's room," Ritchie said. "It is a little small, the room, but very nice — and it has a window that you can open and get fresh air."

Rocket wasn't worried, more like confused. They wanted him to live here — with them?

He noticed a picture on the wall. Ritchie was in a white coat standing in front of a big building.

"Is this a picture of where you work?" Rocket asked.

Ritchie slapped Rocket on the back and laughed loudly. "This is from home, when I was younger. We are from El Salvador. Have you heard of it?"

"It's in Central America," Rocket said, "surrounded by Guatemala, Nicaragua and Honduras."

Ritchie looked shocked.

"I was on the school trivia team for a few years," Rocket said. "I'm a bit of a trivia geek."

"I am very impressed. Young people usually have

not heard of my country, and they never know where it is located."

Rocket pointed a finger gun at Ritchie. "Capital city — San Salvador."

"You are correct. Very good knowledge of geography. We arrive in this country four years ago. It was hard until we learned English — my English is still not so good. But my children speak perfect, and my wife is very good also." He shrugged. "I work as a cleaner for a big company, and I also do the job of superintendent of this building. So, you would like to see the room, yes?"

"Okay," Rocket said, going with it. He'd been imagining his own apartment, but he was used to living with families.

Ritchie led him down a short hallway into the living room. "*Mi amor*, come meet Bryan," Ritchie called out.

A woman came out of the kitchen drying her hands on a dish towel. She was small and slight, like Ritchie, but more delicate looking. Her eyes were striking: a deep blue, with a thin ring of bluish green on the outside. She was pretty, but she looked tired.

She was also oddly familiar. Rocket couldn't place her at first. Then he remembered, the cleaner at the arena, upstairs by the Racers' office.

She offered him a brief smile and seemed to recognize him, too. "We have been talking about taking in a boarder." She spoke with an accent like Ritchie, but her voiçe was softer.

"Bryan is a hockey player. He is playing for the Racers," Ritchie said.

A young boy came running out of a bedroom.

"You play for the Racers? Cool," he said. "What position? Have you played in the NHL? How many goals did you get last year?"

"One question at a time, Rafa," Ritchie said, his eyes dancing. "Please excuse my young son. He is what you call a hockey fanatic."

"That's good. We'll get along then," Rocket said. "I'm a hockey fanatic, too."

"Leona, come say hello," Ritchie said.

Leona peered out of a bedroom, her lips curled in a mischievous smile.

"This is my little angel," Ritchie said. "She has five years."

"Papá, in English you say, 'She is five years old,'" Rafa said. "It's not like in Spanish."

Ritchie laughed. "I am always forgetting. And Rafa is seven years old."

"Good, Papá," Leona said. "That was perfect."

"So, answer my questions," Rafa said to Rocket. He looked ready to explode with excitement.

"Enough, Rafa," his mom said. "Ricardo, you should show Bryan the room."

"Yes, yes, come with me," Ritchie said, pulling Rocket's arm.

He opened the door and Rocket peered inside. It was a small room, not much bigger than a closet, really. The bed took up almost the entire space, but there was a big window. Posters of hockey players covered the walls.

"So, you will stay here," Ritchie said. "Two meals are included in the rent: breakfast and dinner. We are not often here for lunch. The children are at school, and we are working. The rent is $550 a month. Is that fair?"

The other places were two to three times higher, and they didn't come with food — or a bed.

"When would I be able to move in?" Rocket asked. "I'm staying in a hotel right now . . ."

"Oh, that is too much money," said Ritchie. "The room is ready. If you like, you can move in tonight."

Rocket would save a ton of money living here. The location sucked, but so what if he had to take the bus? He was used to it. Ritchie and his family seemed really nice, too. May as well stay here for a while. If he needed to, he could take his time and find something better later.

"Sounds good," Rocket said. "I'll take it."

"Wonderful news," Ritchie proclaimed. "*Mi amor*, Bryan will be taking the room."

"Yay!" Rafa said. "Now can you answer my questions?"

"Shush," his mom said. "Bryan, I won't be here when you return. I must go to work. But we'll have dinner ready for you."

"Thanks, Mi Amor," Rocket said.

Ritchie and the kids began to giggle. He got the feeling he'd said something silly.

"Did I say that wrong?" he said.

Ritchie and the kids burst out laughing. Rafa was laughing so hard, he bent over and held his stomach. Leona draped herself over his back.

"*Mi amor* means 'my love' in Spanish," Ritchie said, finally.

"That's what Papá calls our mamá," Leona said.

"My name is Mariana," her mother said, laughing also.

Rocket joined in. It felt good. Somehow it felt like he hadn't laughed — really laughed — in a long time.

"I'll zip back to the hotel and get my bags — before I say anything else embarrassing," Rocket said as the laughter wound down. "Hopefully, I'll learn a little Spanish while I stay here. How do you say 'I'll see you soon?'"

"Hasta pronto," Leona said.

"Hasta pronto," Rocket repeated. He shook hands with Ritchie and Mariana and left.

He felt ten times better already. While he waited for the bus, he took out his phone and texted his mom the good news.

Is it in a good area? she texted back immediately.

He leaned against the bus shelter and replied: *It's real nice, and so is the family. Don't worry. All good.*

CHAPTER 11

Rocket spun his helmet in his hands. Floyd was never going to shut up. He'd been lecturing them for the past fifteen minutes.

Nadav came into the dressing room. "Coach Mack, Zamboni's almost done. The guys have to be on the ice for the introductions."

Floyd turned to face him, his face twisted in rage. "I'm right in the middle of talking," he roared. "Why don't *you* go on the ice for the introductions?"

Looking confused, Nadav backed up and left.

Rocket had heard that Floyd was a difficult guy — a total jerk was more like it. And obviously not too bright. The team had to hit the ice.

"Who was that?" said the woman next to Floyd.

Rocket had decided she must be Queen Stella — Floyd's wife. She wore a floor-length, tight-fitting red dress, and she was draped in diamonds. Her blond hair fell below her shoulders in soft curls, and her face was heavily made up. Rocket had never seen such long eyelashes.

"He's the trainer," Blywood told her.

"Why we can't hire people born in this country?" Floyd said.

"I believe he's from Pinewood," McGill said.

"I mean his family," Floyd shot back. "Anyway, what was I saying? This is a veteran team, and we don't have an excuse not to win — and we will win. I pay some of the highest salaries in the league, and I expect results. I won't hesitate to make changes if it'll help the club."

Blywood nodded gravely.

"You'll notice that Stephen Strauss isn't here," Floyd said.

Rocket had been wondering.

"He's gone. Say hello to Terrence Day," Floyd said. "We picked Terrence up on waivers. He's a twelve-year AHL veteran. He'll take over centre on Strauss's line."

"Hey, boys. Happy to be on the team," Terrence said.

Rocket hadn't heard of him, so he was fairly sure Terrence had never played in the NHL.

"You don't perform, you're outta here," Floyd said. "We had to let Strauss go — we like guys with experience who don't make dumb mistakes. This is what happens when you lose every faceoff. So, take note. And that goes for each and every one of you. Last year will not be repeated. Do you understand me? We will not lose in the first round again. We will not. That was totally ridiculous."

McGill had his arms crossed, and he was leaning against the wall. He'd barely moved while Floyd ranted. Blywood nodded slowly. Barker had a satisfied smile on his face. Most of Rocket's teammates looked grim.

"You're all too full of yourselves and too full of your NHL dreams. If we don't start winning, you won't be going anywhere. Coach Landry and I talk all the time, like every day, and if you guys jerk me around, you'll be so buried in the minors it would take Sidney Crosby ten years to dig you out. Do we understand each other?"

A few guys murmured, "Yes."

"Good," Floyd said. "This isn't a charity. The play-offs mean money — and I like money. I like to win, too." He pointed at McGill. "Coach Mack, you wanna talk strategy? C'mon, Stella. You have to get ready."

"Sure, Ray-Ray," she cooed. "Bye-bye, boys." She flicked her fingers in a half wave and offered a toothy smile before leaving.

So, Ray-Ray was Stella's pet name for Floyd. The Racers were a strange team.

McGill looked at his watch. "We don't have time for strategy. Play our game and we'll be okay. Hard in the corners and safe with the puck in the first period. You boys know how to play."

The goalies led the players out. Rory hung back with Rocket.

Rocket slapped his friend's pads. "Welcome back to the game," he said.

Rory grinned and slapped Rocket's pads back. "Bring it, bro."

"Bring it."

Rocket held his arm out toward the door. "After you."

Rory went ahead. Rocket breathed a sigh of relief. He had a stupid superstition about being the last player out for a game. He'd been doing it for too long to stop, and he was afraid of what might happen if he did.

The crowd cheered as the Racers came onto the ice, music blasting away. Rocket hopped onto the ice, tore across the red line and made a beeline down the boards. There wasn't much time for a warm-up. The goalie was scraping his crease furiously.

Men began to unroll a red carpet leading from the door to centre. Then Floyd and Stella walked out. The horn sounded, and Rocket headed to the bench. He was on the fourth line, so he went to sit in the middle. Barker was behind him. Time to try Rory's advice.

"Hey, Coach, any pointers for my first game? I got to admit I'm a bit nervous, and you have a lot of experience—"

"You want some advice?" Barker said. "Rookies should shut up and do their jobs."

Rocket's stomach sank. Barker moved away to talk to Kaufman. That sure hadn't worked. Wrong time, probably. Stupid to ask right before a game. He'd work him at practice. Right now, it was time to show he was a good teammate.

"Let's go, Racers," he said loudly. "Our puck all game."

Rory was starting with C.C. and Goldsy. They were standing across the Racers' blue line.

"Please join international recording star Stella Getty-Floyd in the singing of our national anthem," the announcer said.

Rocket stood up. Stella started to sing.

He looked around to see if this was a joke. She was terrible. How could she be a star? He sang better than that — and he couldn't sing. The players kept it together, aside from a few smirks. When she was done, the crowd let loose with a huge cheer. Rocket figured they were clapping because it was over.

"Now, we'll have the ceremonial dropping of the puck to mark the forty-first season the Racers have been part of the Floyd family. We're honoured to have in attendance Racers president, chief executive officer and executive general manager Raymond Floyd," the announcer said.

C.C. and the Ravens' captain skated to centre. Floyd dropped the puck. C.C. pulled it to his skate, took off his glove, picked it up and gave it to Stella. She gave him and the other captain big hugs. Both captains shook Floyd's hand. Floyd and Stella walked back along the red carpet, waving to the crowd. The music started up, and the crowd began chanting, *"Go, Racers, go! Go, Racers, go!"*

Rocket's two wingers were sitting next to him. Turner Rogers was a right winger. Brett Downey was on the left. Both were second-year guys. Rocket didn't know much about them, other than they seemed like good players. Rogers had been a fairly high draft pick, maybe even a second-rounder. He could really skate, and he had a nice shot. He was also a big body and seemed to like the rough stuff. Downey wasn't the greatest skater, but he played with an edge, full out, had a wicked shot — and he liked to take the body, too. Rocket wondered why they were on the fourth line.

"Let's go hard," Rocket said to break the tension.

Rogers gave him a cold look. "I got a text from Straussy before the game," he said to Downey. "Looks like he's going to clear waivers."

"That sucks," Downey said. "He got a raw deal. The guy's a winger. He steps up and plays centre and gets burned because of his faceoffs."

"Can't believe they're going with Terrence Day," Rogers said quietly. "I've got nothing against the guy, but . . . he's a bit old. Straussy can skate circles around him."

Rocket grabbed a water bottle and took a long sip. If they were right about Terrence, then Rocket had a good chance of moving up to third line.

If so, then he needed to make that happen soon.

CHAPTER 12

Rocket looked up at the scoreboard. The game was almost over, with seven minutes left in the third.

They'd gotten off to a good start, when C.C. got a quick goal in the first period. Rory had pounded in a rebound off a point shot to make it 2–0 late in the second. Less positive — Rocket's line had only been out for three shifts all game.

Coach McGill had told them to bring some energy, and that's what Rocket tried to do. He managed to land a good hit in the neutral zone, and he even got a shot on net. It was from a bad angle, but at least he'd made the goalie react.

A few fans began to chant, *"Go, Racers, go!"* Rocket looked around for them. Then, for the second time since he'd come to Pinewood, he had a good laugh. The four boys who'd been in the Honda Civic were three rows up behind the bench. He hadn't noticed them before, so he figured they must have snuck down to the expensive seats. They were hard to miss. Crawford and Chaz had painted their faces yellow and black, and Rino and Griff wore tinfoil Stanley Cup hats.

Tweet. The referee pointed to the penalty box — tripping.

"Buy yourself some new glasses, Stripes," Crawford called out.

"You've disappointed me for the last time!" Chaz shouted.

"Total dive!" Crawford yelled. "He flopped like a fish. Look, he's laughing at you."

The boys were so into it, it was hilarious. Crawford started falling all over the place to make his point.

Beauclair headed to the penalty box.

"Take the kill for thirty seconds," Kaufman said.

Rocket wondered who he was talking to.

"Rockwood, are you deaf?" Barker shouted. "He said get out there. C.C. needs a breather." He pulled Rocket up by his shoulder pads.

Rocket forced his stiff legs to hop over the boards. He almost wished he didn't have to play. Brutal to take a shift after watching for so long. To make it worse, the faceoff was in the Racers' end, to the goalie's right.

The crowd clapped to the music. The referee blew his whistle, and the music stopped. The Ravens' centre was a big guy. He was lined up slightly on the inside. Rocket figured he was trying to give himself space to pull it back to the defenceman for a quick shot from the top of the circle.

"He's yours," Rocket said to Goldsy, nodding to the defenceman.

"Just win it back," Goldsy growled.

Rocket flushed and bent down for the faceoff. Sure, rookies don't tell vets what to do. But as centre, it was his job to make sure everyone knew what they had to do after the draw.

The puck dropped. Their sticks flashed — Rocket's a touch faster. The puck slid to the corner. His defence-man retrieved it and headed around the net. Rocket drifted to the slot. That felt good. A clean win, late in the third, on a critical draw in their own end.

The defenceman fired it up the wall.

Rocket groaned. The puck clipped the linesman's skate and stayed in. Goldsy and the Ravens' right defenceman arrived at the puck at the same time. The defenceman tied Goldsy up, while his right winger dug the puck out. He turned and drifted backwards toward the blue line.

"I got him," Goldsy called out.

Rocket stayed in the high slot, keeping a wary eye on the left defenceman in case he tried to sneak down low. The Ravens' right winger held the puck until Goldsy got close, and then he flipped it to the right defenceman, who had stayed at the hash marks against the boards. The left defenceman took off, and Rocket turned and got a stick on him to slow him down. The defenceman stopped and went back to the point.

Rocket felt good about that defensive play. The right defenceman gave the puck to the winger at the point, and Rocket drifted back to the high slot. He had a feeling the Ravens' winger and defenceman were uncomfortable having switched positions. He bet they'd move the puck to the other side of the ice so they could switch back. Rocket snuck a quick look behind him. The Racers defence were doing a good job keeping the Ravens from setting up in front of the net. Rocket cheated a few steps toward the point and hoped the Ravens would make a mistake.

The winger held the puck, his head up looking for an open man. He faked a pass to the right defenceman. Goldsy extended his stick to cut that off. The right defenceman backed up into the corner. The Racers' left defenceman took a few steps in that direction also. Rocket waited. It was going to happen. He knew it. The winger was getting nervous about holding the puck so long. The winger took another quick look down the wall — and then he passed it across the blue line to the left defenceman.

Rocket was on the left defenceman like a shot. The left defenceman didn't even try to control it. Instead, he chipped it to the boards to Rocket's right and retreated from the line. Rocket cut over to the right to snare the puck off the boards and headed up-ice, Goldsy with him on the left.

A two-on-one on the penalty kill. Rocket tried to keep his emotions in check. They needed to make this count.

"Rockwood, change!" Barker screamed.

Rocket hesitated.

"Change!"

Rocket passed to Goldsy and headed to the bench. He heard a groan and turned in time to see the Ravens with the puck storming into the Racers' zone. C.C. flew over the boards. Goldsy came back over next, and Rory took his spot.

"Where'd you go?" Goldsy said to Rocket angrily. "I passed back to you."

"Barker called me off," Rocket said.

Goldsy's expression changed. "Okay . . . But next time, tell me," he said.

Rocket made his way to the middle of the bench and sat next to Rogers. The Ravens had control of the puck to the goalie's left at the half-boards.

Barker grabbed Rocket by the inside edge of his shoulder pads. "You don't abandon a guy on a two-on-one. Have you ever played before? You cost us a chance at a short-handed goal, and now look — the puck's back in our end."

The Ravens got a shot on net from the point. The goalie kicked it to the corner with a pad save. Rory retrieved the puck, whirled, and lofted the puck over the defence and down the ice. Rocket closed his eyes and leaned his head back. At least they hadn't scored.

He felt a glove tap his leg.

"He called you off," Rogers said gruffly.

"Umm, yeah. Maybe I should've stayed on . . ." Rocket managed.

Rogers shrugged. "Maybe he shouldn't have called you off."

"He's a doorknob," Downey said. "Who calls for a change on a two-on-one? So dumb."

Both of them looked away. Rocket didn't follow up. He felt better. At least two of the guys had heard Barker, and they didn't seem to like him, either. But it was clear Barker wasn't going to let up on Rocket, and he had all of the power.

It seemed like Barker was winning this battle, but Rocket intended to win the war. Though, at this point, he had no idea how.

CHAPTER 13

Rocket glided over to the boards, dragging his right skate behind him. Usually his nerves were going crazy before a game. But if the Ravens game was any indication, his line wouldn't see much ice time tonight. This was a three-line team. Too bad, too: he'd gotten Ritchie and the kids some tickets. They were good seats — just up behind the players' bench.

Then Rocket had an idea.

He grabbed a puck off the bench and hopped up to talk to them.

"How do you like the view?" he said.

"They're awesome seats," Rafa said, his eyes bright and full of joy. "It's like we're on the ice."

Rocket laughed. "We could use you. The Marlies are a good team."

"Show him the sign," Ritchie said.

Leona and Rafa unrolled a banner.

We ♥ The Rocket

"That's great, guys! Thanks." He felt bad they wouldn't have much reason to show it. "That deserves a puck." Rocket tossed one to Rafa.

"What about me?" Leona said.

"I'll get you one after the game," Rocket said. "A brand-new one."

"I want a brand-new one, too," Rafa said.

"That one is just as special," Ritchie said. "It's been used by real players." He laughed. "Now say thank you, and let Bryan get back to his game."

"Thanks, Rocket Man!" the kids chorused.

Rocket waved and they sat back down in their seats.

"Is that the famous Bryan 'The Rocket' Rockwood?"

"Megan? You didn't tell me you were coming."

She stood up on a seat so she could lean over the glass. "André and Maddy wanted to surprise you, and at the last second they couldn't come. So, I thought I'd just drive up and watch."

"Tell me next time. I could've scored some tickets," he said.

She held up her ticket stub. "I managed to score my own. Have a great game. Can we meet for a bit after?"

"Sure. Wait in the lobby." He heard the Zamboni coming on. "Got to get ready. Sorry," he said.

"Bring it," she mouthed.

He laughed and headed back across the ice to the dressing room.

"Yo, Rocket. Big game, bro," Crawford called. He was leaning over the overhead railing, and he held out his hand as Rocket came under it.

Rocket gave it a slap with his glove.

"Tell McGill to get you on the power play," Chaz said.

"I'll try," Rocket said with a grin.

"Kiss the cup, bro," Crawford said.

Rino lowered his tinfoil Stanley Cup hat. Rocket felt silly, but he gave it a peck. The boys let out a huge whoop.

Griff dangled his scarf, and Rocket gave it a tug as he went by. He was still chuckling at their antics as he opened the dressing-room door.

"I'm glad the game is such a joke," Barker said to him.

Rocket forced a smile. He took his spot next to Rory.

"Can you grab me some water?" Rory asked. He was stretching his right leg, and he looked to be in a bit of pain.

Rocket went over to the far wall, filled a cup and handed it to him.

Rory nodded in thanks and popped something in his mouth. He finished the water. "Don't know why, but the knee's tightened up on me," he said. He stretched his leg out again and put a bottle in his backpack. Then he slapped Rocket's thigh. "I think you're going to have a big game tonight."

"You mean, I might be on for a whole shift?" Rocket joked.

"He can't go with three lines the entire year, especially not with Terrence Day as the third centre. He doesn't have the fitness or the speed," Rory said in a low voice. "Some of the guys think McGill's nervous about getting fired, so he wants to put some wins together to buy himself some time. That's why he's double-shifting C.C. so much. Floyd thinks we have a championship team. I'm not sure."

"Winning is the name of the game," Rocket said.

"Yeah, but Floyd doesn't strike me as a guy who'd

recognize talent if it hit him in the face. I'm only here because I know Kaufman from way back. I mean, why bring Day in? Strauss is a good winger. He's just not a centre. And if they keep double-shifting C.C., he's going to wear down. You wait and see. It's a long season, and he can't play every power play and penalty kill, plus take a regular shift — not with only three lines. No one can."

"Listen up, ladies," Barker said. "Mr. Floyd wants to talk to you."

Rory stretched his leg out. He took a deep breath.

"Good win in the opener," Floyd said. "I thought the goal they scored was a bit soft."

"Total gimme," Barker said.

"I wasn't totally thrilled with the effort level, either," Floyd continued. "Guys who don't pay the price won't be here too long."

C.C. stayed silent, but his eyes flashed angrily. Most of the guys had their heads down. Rory continued to massage his knee.

"That puck is ours — every shift," Floyd said. "We grind it out and play physical."

"True dat," Barker said.

Rocket spun his helmet in his hands. He needed to make something happen when his chance came, even if it was one shift. He needed to get noticed. It would also be nice to show Ritchie and the kids — and Megan — a little something.

Nadav came in. "Zamboni is almost off. Ref told me we're ready."

Floyd threw his hands in the air. "This kid is an interrupting machine. I guess you didn't notice I was talking again?"

Nadav swallowed heavily. "Sorry, Mr. Floyd. Coach McGill asked me to tell him when—"

"Guess they don't teach manners in your country," Floyd said.

"This *is* my country," Nadav said, not backing down this time.

Floyd snorted in disgust. "Whatever. Mack, get these boys fired up. I want a win tonight." He spun on his heel and left.

McGill looked around the room slowly. His eyes burned brightly. "You heard the man — win."

"All right, let's go," Barker yelled, clapping a few times.

The goalies led them out. Rory did a couple of knee bends.

"Did it loosen up?" Rocket said.

"Yeah . . . Maybe I was dehydrated," Rory said. "I got to remember to drink more water. Remind me, okay?"

"Yeah, sure," Rocket said.

Rory was acting kind of weird, like he was embarrassed about something. Rocket figured he didn't like to draw attention to his knee.

They punched gloves and Rory headed out. Rocket waited until all the players were gone.

"You heard the man," Rocket said to himself. "Win."

He went down the hallway. He could hear the crowd cheering. Ritchie, Rafa, Leona, Megan, they were all out there to cheer for him.

It was time to prove he could do better than fourth line in the AHL.

CHAPTER 14

Tweet!

C.C.'s shoulders slumped, and he skated to the bench. McGill had been double-shifting him all game, and he looked exhausted.

"Faceoff in their zone," Barker said. "Suck it up, C.C."

C.C.'s face was pale. "Tweaked my groin. I got to stretch it out."

"What a year," McGill huffed. "This is all I need." He looked down the bench.

Kaufman leaned over and said something to him.

"Rockwood, take C.C.'s spot until we figure this out," McGill said.

"Look alive for once, Rockwood, and don't do anything stupid," Barker said to him. "Pull the puck back to the point, then go look for a rebound."

Rogers and Downey stared glumly at their skates. Rocket felt bad. He knew how much they wanted to play. It had been killing him to just watch, too.

Rocket hopped the boards and darted to the faceoff on the goalie's left.

"You got this," Rory said. He settled into his right-wing spot against the boards.

"Is Beauclair hurt, too?" Goldsy said. He looked over to the bench.

The referee blasted his whistle. The linesman squatted and held the puck out. Rocket quickly adopted a reverse grip. No time to assess the other centre. He'd have to play it straight. Barker was right. Pull it back to his defenceman, then charge the net.

"You got this," Rory said, louder this time.

Rocket shot him a puzzled glance. Rory nodded to the corner. He wanted Rocket to punch it there to set up a cycle. The centre put his stick down. Decision time. Play it safe or try Rory's idea? Rocket switched to a regular grip and put his stick down — when had listening to Barker ever paid off?

The puck dropped. Rocket whacked it into the corner. Rory slipped past the defenceman and collected it. The centre turned and dropped to one knee. Rory saucered the puck over the guy's stick to Rocket, who took it at the faceoff dot.

Goldsy pushed against the defenceman in front of the net and held his stick out for a pass. Rocket took a step forward. The left winger threw himself to the ice, and the goalie dropped into his butterfly.

Instinct took over. Rocket faked a pass to Goldsy, and in the same motion, he let loose a wicked snap shot over the goalie's shoulder.

He gasped. Someone had cross-checked him from behind. For a moment, the air left his body and he struggled to breathe.

"Bush-league cheap shot!" Rory yelled.

A defenceman stood in his way. Rory pushed him back, trying to get to the guy who'd hit Rocket.

"I got him," the referee said.

Rocket sat up.

The referee pointed at the centreman. "You're gone for two minutes: a cross-check after the play."

The centre groaned. "I barely touched him. He's two inches tall. Not my fault he fell like a house of cards."

Rocket got up on one knee. "I learned that trick from Thumbelina," he said.

The centre rolled his eyes and headed to the box.

Rocket stood up. The puck must have deflected out of play. He wondered where the faceoff was.

Then Rory came over with the puck in hand. "An honour to get an assist on your first AHL goal," he said.

It took a moment to register. "That actually went in? A goal?"

Rory slapped his shin pads. "I think that's what they call it when this little black thingy goes in between those red posty things."

Rocket rolled his shoulders and neck. That cross-check had really hurt. He felt a bit wobbly.

Rory handed him the puck. "Welcome to the league — and way to pay the price in close."

Goldsy tapped Rocket's pads. "Nice shot," he said simply, then skated away.

Rocket's two defencemen gave him a pat on the helmet and skated back to the Racers' blue line.

Suddenly, Rocket was overcome by a dizzy spell. He closed his eyes and shook his head. The feeling went away, but he still felt a bit sick to his stomach.

Nadav leaned over the boards. "Are you okay? That was a nasty hit."

Rocket skated over and gave Nadav the puck.

"I'm fi—"

"Give me a break," Barker interrupted. "He barely got touched." He leaned over the boards, too. "Rockwood, don't think I didn't notice you disobeying my order on that faceoff. And don't think scoring made up for it." He stood back up on the bench.

"It was a nice shot," Nadav said to him.

Rocket grunted and went to centre. McGill was keeping him on. That was the important thing, not Barker's stupid comments.

He leaned down for the draw. Again, a wave of dizziness flooded over him and dots danced in his eyes. He blinked a few times and took a deep breath. The referee dropped the puck. Rocket swung his stick mechanically. The puck skidded back to his left defenceman.

Rocket did a quick curl and took a short pass on the fly. He crossed centre and gave it up to Rory, who continued down the wall. The other team's left defenceman stumbled slightly, and Rory was able to keep going.

Just over the blue line Rory cut inside, and Rocket crossed behind him to the boards. Rory rewarded him with a nice backhand flip pass. The Marlies' defenceman kept with Rory, confident his winger could track Rocket down.

Rocket felt a slash on his right leg at the top of the circle. The winger wasn't able to keep up — they didn't call him the Rocket for nothing!

He took it on net. The goalie came out to challenge. The left defenceman broke away from Rory and came across to head off Rocket.

Looking over his shoulder, Rocket saw Goldsy cruising into the zone, watched closely by the right winger. The centre had hustled back and had a stick on Rory.

Rocket faked a backhander to Goldsy, then made an unexpected power move on goal. The defenceman was surprised by his explosiveness, and Rocket was able to gain the edge. The goalie dropped into a butterfly a half-metre in front of his crease. He wasn't giving Rocket much to shoot at, but Rocket figured any shot was better than nothing. He lowered his left hand and let the backhander go. The puck was still flying when the defenceman launched himself into Rocket's back.

For a horrible second, Rocket thought he would crash into the post. His chest grazed the iron, and he tumbled to the ice behind the net, his momentum carrying him hard into the boards.

He heard a siren, and the crowd begin cheering loudly. Rocket looked at the net. The puck was nestled in the corner. Rory was holding his stick over his head in victory. He skated over to Rocket.

"Did you get a rebound?" Rocket asked, blinking a few times. He felt unsteady.

"Nope. All you. It was off the goalie's mask and in," Rory said. "My honour to assist on your second AHL goal — *this shift!*"

He helped Rocket up, then pounded him on the back of the helmet. Rocket wished he hadn't. It made him even dizzier, and it hurt his neck. Goldsy and the defencemen joined in the celebration, and they all patted his helmet. Rocket almost fell. What was wrong with him?

Beauclair's line had come out. Rocket gladly went to the bench. He needed some water. The guys were nice enough to hold out their gloves as he side-stepped his way to the middle, next to Rogers and Downey.

"Nice work," Rogers said.

Downey reached a glove out and Rocket punched it.

When Rocket leaned forward to get some water, the spots came back. He waited for them to disappear. Weird. It was like he was fine one minute, and then he could barely stand up. He took a sip of water. It burned the back of his throat.

Nadav tapped him on the shoulder. "Bryan, can I run a few tests on you?"

"What for?" Rocket said.

"Have you had any dizziness or pain in the head or neck since that cross-check?" Nadav said. He was testing Rocket for a concussion.

The last thing Rocket needed was to start the third period alone in the dark room, especially after scoring two goals. He had to stay in the game. "Not really. It hurt, though," he said.

"Where are you?" Nadav said.

"On the bench," Rocket said.

"No. I mean, name the building."

Rocket hesitated. The name had somehow slipped his mind. "It's called . . . I just moved here so . . ." Then it came to him. "Pinewood Barns Arena," he said with relief.

"What day of the week is it?"

"It's . . . Sunday," Rocket said. He had to dig deep for that one.

"What city are you in?"

"Pinewood."

"Repeat these five words: table, dog, green, boat, shoe."

Rocket repeated them.

"Do you remember the hit?"

"It was the last shift. Rory passed to me."

"What was the score before you got your first goal?"

It was close. He knew that. Rocket looked up at the scoreboard: 2–0. He'd just gotten two goals so . . . he gave his head a shake. He was being stupid. "Zero, all."

"What were the five words I asked you to repeat?"

Rocket was stumped. "Green . . . Um, I wasn't really listening."

Barker came over. He didn't look happy.

"Goldsy needs a new stick," he told Nadav. "Leave Rockwood alone. I told you he's fine."

"He took a hit to the back of the head or possibly the neck," Nadav said softly. "I'm worried about a concussion."

"Come on," Barker said. "When did hockey become a game for little boys who need their mommies?"

"Protocol is that we—"

"C.C. is out with a pulled groin," Barker cut Nadav off savagely. "We've only got three centres. He's fine. Look at him. He's totally okay. Rockwood, you're okay to play, right?" He glared down at Rocket.

"I'm good," Rocket said.

"Told you. Now get that stick for Goldsy and then check on C.C.," Barker said. He turned back to the ice. "Call the hook, ref!" he yelled.

"Tell me if you get a headache or your neck hurts — or if you see spots or become sensitive to light,"

Nadav said. He patted Rocket's shoulder pads and left.

"Pick up the physical play, little boys," Barker said. "We need to crush their spirit."

"I wouldn't mind crushing his spirit with my physical play," Rogers whispered to Downey.

Downey chuckled.

Rocket contented himself with a long sip of water. Barker wasn't winning any friends on the team. He was a rookie coach, and as he himself had said, *"Rookies should shut up and do their jobs."*

CHAPTER 15

The coaching staff, along with Floyd and Blywood, crowded around C.C. in the dressing room after the game.

Rocket put on his sweatshirt. He'd already showered and dressed.

"I told you not to overuse him," Floyd said to McGill.

"We'll monitor the situation for a few days," McGill replied.

"The playing minutes should've been managed better," Barker said.

"Exactly," Floyd said.

Rocket felt bad for McGill. Floyd didn't seem to like him too much.

"You want to come for a workout tomorrow morning?" Rory asked Rocket.

"Definitely," Rocket said.

Not actually true. Right now, all he wanted to do was sleep for a week. But if Rory was working out — and he'd played in the NHL — then Rocket should, too.

"See you tomorrow, nine o'clock," Rory said. "Good game, bro. Two goals and an assist — awesome."

In the third period, Rocket had stayed on the first line with Goldsy and Rory. He'd gotten an assist on Goldsy's one-time slapshot from the top of the circle.

Rocket said goodbye to Rory and went to the door.

"Good game," Goldsy called out to him.

"Oh . . . th-thanks," Rocket stuttered. "Good game to you. Too."

Goldsy turned to talk to Rory.

Rocket wondered about himself sometimes. He'd sounded ridiculous. Nice of Goldsy, though. Maybe Rocket had made a good impression today — a real step toward being accepted on the team.

"Aren't you forgetting something?" Nadav said to him at the door.

"Don't think so," Rocket said.

"Didn't you have your first of these tonight?"

Rocket had no idea what he was talking about.

Nadav gave him an odd look as he pulled a puck out of his pocket. "Your first goal? This is the puck." He held it up. There it was, in gold lettering, the date and *Bryan Rockwood, 1st AHL Goal.*

"You're the best!" Rocket said, reaching for it. "I'd almost forgotten." In truth, he was having a hard time remembering the actual goal.

"I want to check you out tomorrow. I know it's an off day, but is there any chance you can come by?" Nadav said.

"I'm working out with Rory at . . . in the morning." Rocket couldn't remember what time Rory had said.

"I'll see you then," Nadav said.

"Hey, you," Floyd yelled from across the room. "Get me a bottle of water. I'm parched here."

Nadav grimaced before reaching for a bottle. Rocket didn't envy him.

As he headed to the lobby, Rocket got more excited with each step. Cool that Megan had seen his first goal — his first two. And he was glad Ritchie and the kids had been there, too.

The lights in the lobby were bright, and he had to put a hand across his eyes. His head swam, and he leaned against the wall.

The feeling passed almost as fast as it came, but Rocket was unnerved all the same. He felt good. He did. So, was it a concussion? The symptoms — dizziness, nausea, forgetfulness, sensitivity to light — seemed to come and go.

After a game like tonight's, an injury would be an epic disaster. He'd finally had the chance to prove he could play. Plus, C.C. was going to be out for a least a few games. The team needed Rocket, and he didn't want to let them down.

Leona saw him first. "There's Rocket Man!" she shrieked.

She and Rafa hopped up and down, their hands over their heads.

"Hey, guys," Rocket said. "Enjoy the game?"

"We very much enjoyed your goals," Ritchie said.

"Did you get my puck?" Leona said.

He'd forgotten. Rocket felt the puck in his pocket — his first AHL goal. "Of course, I did," he said. He gave it a last look and handed it to her.

"Mine doesn't have writing," Rafa wailed.

"You can share them," Rocket said.

"This is mine," Leona said to Rafa.

"Not fair," Rafa whined.

"Children can be a great joy in life — and a great big headache," Ritchie said, laughing.

Megan spotted him. "Great game, Bryan. Wow! So glad I came. André and Maddy will be mad they missed it. Two goals! That was a dirty hit, though. He should've been kicked out."

Rocket rubbed the back of his neck. "Tell me about it. I was seeing spots there for a while."

"Do you think you have a concussion?" she said.

"Megan, have you met my Pinewood family?" Rocket said quickly. "Ritchie, Rafa and Leona."

"Bryan gave me a puck with writing on it," Leona said.

Rafa scowled deeply.

"I'll write on your puck, too," Rocket told him.

Rafa stuck his tongue out at Leona, and she stuck hers out back.

"I am Ritchie. Very nice to meet a friend of Bryan," Ritchie said.

Megan smiled at him. "Nice to meet you, too."

"We should get going," said Ritchie. "Our bus will be here soon. We will see you at home, Bryan."

"I can give you a ride," Megan offered.

"It is okay. You have a long drive home," Ritchie said.

"It's no problem," Megan said. "I can fit five people."

Rocket was too tired to turn down a lift. "Once

85

Megan decides something, you won't get her to change her mind," he said. "Let's get these two brats home."

"He's the brat," Leona said, pointing at Rafa. "I'm a wonderful child."

Megan laughed, and they all headed to the door, the two kids chattering away.

Rafa and Leona kept at it all the way home, with Megan and Ritchie laughing the entire time. Rocket had trouble following the conversation, and he was so drained from the game, he could barely keep his eyes open.

Megan pulled over in front of their building.

"Again, thank you," Ritchie said. "I hope you will be able to return for a long visit soon. I think Bryan will be lonely here without his friends or family."

"I will, thanks. Hopefully soon. School is busy, but I'll figure out another game, maybe on a Friday or Saturday."

"Wonderful. I will be looking forward to it," Ritchie said. He and the two kids got out.

"Bye, guys," Megan said. "Take care of Bryan for me."

"I'll be home in a bit," Rocket told them.

He yawned deeply as they left.

"Am I that dull?" Megan joked.

"No. Sorry. Just tired for some reason," Rocket said.

"So . . . how are things going? André told me about this coach of yours, Barker? He sounds like a real jerk. What if he keeps giving you a hard time?"

"I can deal with him. No worries." He yawned again.

"You've yawned about ten times since we left the rink," Megan said. "I think that guy messed you up a bit."

"I'm fine. Honest. I was just up early today." It was all he could do to keep his eyes open.

Megan ran her hand through her hair. "Have you registered for those online courses yet?"

Rocket looked out the window. "Not yet. I will. It's been busy."

"This is serious, Bryan. What if you get hurt and can't play? You'll have nothing to fall back on."

"I could point out that no one on my team is taking courses. We're professional hockey players."

"I'm not saying full-time, obviously — but a course a semester?"

He couldn't stop another yawn.

Megan leaned forward. "You know, you really might have a concussion. You're exhausted, and you looked a bit unsteady back at the rink."

"Okay, Doctor Megan. Calm down. It was just a hit. I'm good. Watch." He touched his nose quickly with his index fingers.

He stopped. He'd begun to feel dizzy. "I don't have a concussion, and even if I do, it's not a bad one."

"They're all bad," Megan said.

"Listen, Megan. C.C., the team captain, is hurt. I might get to play on the first line or at least move up to the second if they replace him with Beauclair. They'll never move Terrence Day up. This is my chance to prove myself to Coach Mack and Floyd. This is huge. I can't risk it by sitting out a bunch of games because I yawned a few times."

"It's not worth your health."

He felt himself get mad. "I have no choice. Hockey players play hurt."

"You always have a choice."

"We need the money. I have to do this."

"You think your mom and Maddy want you to risk your brain for hockey?"

"Stop exaggerating — and please, don't tell them. I'm fine. I don't want them to worry about me."

Megan took a deep breath. "Can you at least get checked out?"

"I will. We have an off day tomorrow."

"Go inside," Megan said. "You're tired and . . . you should get to sleep."

He sighed. "Sorry. You came all the way here."

"It's late, and it's a long drive. I should go, too," she said.

He really was exhausted. "Are you sure?"

"Go to bed. That's an order."

Rocket got out.

"Please don't tell my mom or Maddy," he said.

"As long as you go to the doctor," she said.

He nodded wearily and closed the door. She drove away.

The ground seemed to rush toward him. He held his arms out to steady himself and took a few deep breaths until the feeling went away. Then he walked inside, no problem.

He didn't have a concussion.

He couldn't.

Not now.

CHAPTER 16

Rocket walked along the sidewalk. He was exhausted, despite passing out the second his head hit the pillow the night before. He'd even overslept. But he was still too tired to hurry, even though he was running late to meet Rory.

He remembered he'd told Megan he'd go to the doctor. It was nice that she worried about him; he honestly appreciated it. She just didn't know what it took to make it to the NHL, not really. She didn't get the sacrifice, the pain.

Rocket went into the arena. The workout room was in the basement. He headed across the lobby to the staircase.

"The floor just got washed!" the arena manager yelled at him. "Who are you, anyway?"

"I'm Bryan . . . Rockwood. I'm with the Racers."

"Oh. Well, okay. Use the side entrance from now on, please. I've told Blywood a thousand times. You guys keep messing the floors up."

"Sorry," Rocket said. "I didn't know."

"Clean up his footprints," the man yelled at a

woman holding a mop and wearing a yellow uniform with a baseball cap.

Mariana.

Rocket was instantly furious at the manager, but Mariana shook her head at him as she wrung the mop out in the pail. She didn't want Rocket to say anything.

"Hurry up. You still have to sweep the upper level," the man said to her. "The concert starts at seven, so we need to cover the ice, put the chairs out and set up the stage."

"Yes, sir," Mariana said.

"And clean Mr. Floyd's office again when you're done," he said.

"We did it yesterday, sir," she said.

"He wants it done again," he snapped. "What a day. I'm doing everything myself, as usual." He stomped off.

"Sorry about the footprints, Mariana," Rocket said. "Let me mop. It's my fault."

"It's fine. Don't mind him," she said. "He yells all the time about everything. I have learned not to listen. I just say 'yes, sir' and do my job. I think he's scared of Mr. Floyd."

"He's not the only one," Rocket said.

"Do you have a practice?" Mariana said.

"No. I'm working out."

"Thank you again for the tickets. It was such a nice treat. Ricardo told me the kids had a wonderful time — and they love their pucks."

"Anytime they want to go, just let me know."

The arena manager came back. "Are you going to clean the floor?" he cried.

"Sorry, sir." Mariana began to mop furiously.

"Can I *help* you?" the man said to Rocket.

"No. I'm going to the workout room," he replied, but he couldn't keep the edge out of his voice. Even though Mariana didn't want him to interfere, it was hard to be nice to a guy who treated his employees like that. He wished Mariana didn't have to work for him.

Rocket hurried down the stairs and along the hall. He heard the clinking of weights. Rory had beaten him — naturally. As he walked in, he could see Nadav was there, too.

"You slacking off because of two lousy goals?" Rory asked Rocket. He did a squat.

"I slept in. Sorry."

"No excuses," Rory grunted. He did another squat. "You'll do an extra circuit to make up for it."

"What are you doing today?" Rocket asked.

"Squats, push-ups, bench jumps, burpees," Rory said. "Why don't you warm up, and you can follow me."

Rory did a final squat and Nadav took the barbell from his shoulders.

Rocket peeled off his sweatshirt and track pants. "Are you here to work out, too, Nadav?"

"No, I came in to check on you, remember? How are you feeling?"

Rocket had forgotten. "Fine . . . I was tired last night. Not used to the ice time, I guess. I'm good now, though."

Rory began to do push-ups.

"Were you dizzy at any time?" Nadav said. He came closer and looked into Rocket's eyes.

"Nah. I'm fine. Seriously."

"Stand on one foot and hold your arms out, shoulder height."

"I told you—"

"Do it."

Rocket felt silly. Nadav led him through a series of balancing drills and eye-hand coordination exercises.

"Now touch your nose, alternating each hand."

Rocket did it.

"Turn around three times and stand on your left leg."

Rocket managed that.

"Okay, you're done," Nadav said.

"How'd I do?" Rocket said.

Nadav pressed his lips together and looked into Rocket's eyes again. "Concussions are tricky things to diagnose. Have you ever had one before?"

"No, I don't think so."

"Sometimes you can get dizzy and suffer concussion-like symptoms from a blow to the neck or back," Nadav said. "Any sensitivity to light?"

Rocket looked up at the ceiling lights. "A bit after the game, but not now."

"My bet is you have a minor concussion," Nadav said. "You should have it seen by a doctor to confirm it."

Rocket thought of his promise to Megan. She'd wanted him to get checked out by a doctor, but Nadav seemed to know what he was doing. And Rocket was feeling better, except for being tired.

Rory finished a set of burpees. "Your call, Rocket, but if you see a doctor, they'll probably make you sit out a few games to be on the safe side. You know what doctors are like. This might not be the best time to shut things down, not with C.C. on the shelf."

"We're talking about the brain here," Nadav said.

"I know, and I'm not saying head injuries aren't serious," Rory said. "And like I said before, you got to take care of your body. But it's hard to shake a reputation for concussions. It's different if you're already an NHLer. Like I said, it's up to you, Bryan, but if you feel okay, then I'd chance it. If you feel gross and dizzy, then for sure get it checked out."

Rocket began to roll his shoulders back. "I appreciate this, Nadav. I'm good. If the symptoms come back, I'll go to the doctor. I will. I have a chance to play — and I can't afford to miss any games."

Nadav shrugged. "I'll be keeping an eye on you. If you're having any problems, then I need to report them."

A phone rang.

"Shoot," Rory said. He did a squat. "I bet that's Melissa. I forgot to tell her we'd be working out now. Excuse me, boys," He put the barbell down and dug his phone out of his bag. "Hi, honey, how are you?" He stepped into the hall.

Rocket began to stretch his legs.

"He's a dedicated player," Nadav said.

"Sure is. Hope the knee holds up."

"This game takes a physical toll on you," Nadav said. "Got to wonder if it's worth it."

Hockey required sacrifice. But how much was too much? Rocket did a few sit-ups.

"I'll take some weights off for the squats," Nadav said.

"It's fine. I'll use his," Rocket said. He stood up.

"He's a bit bigger than you."

"Looks okay to me."

Nadav helped him put the barbell across his shoulders. It was heavy.

"One . . . two . . . three . . ." Nadav counted.

Rocket's legs were burning. "How many does Rory do?" he managed.

"He does ten, but why don't you start with five?" Nadav said.

"Four . . . five."

Nadav took the barbell. Rocket felt weak all over. That was a ton of weight. But if Rory did it, then he had to do it. He had to do even more.

CHAPTER 17

Rocket waited for the bus. He was completely drained after the workout — and he'd barely managed two circuits. Rory had done five.

A car stopped beside him.

"Awesome game, Rocket," Crawford said through the passenger window. He twisted in his seat. Across the back of his Racers sweater, in white lettering, was *ROCKWOOD*.

"Nice styling," Rocket said.

Rino leaned over from the driver's seat and waved his Racers hat. Griff whirled his scarf. Chaz tapped the logo on his Racers sweater. These guys were superfans.

"How're the boys doing today?" Rocket said.

"Totally psyched after last night's game," Crawford said. "Massive goals, bro. Massive. Huge win. You ready for tomorrow's game?"

"Hope so."

"Huge four-game road trip coming up," Chaz said.

"Definitely," Rocket said. "C.C. may be a little banged up, so we'll see how it goes."

"You staying on the first line?" Chaz asked.

"You and Rory Colbert are a good pair," Crawford said.

Rocket loved these guys. It was hockey 24/7, just the way it should be.

"Not sure where I'm playing. C.C. is day-to-day. Hopefully, he can go on. Rory's a great player, though. I love playing with him. Big body, smart with the puck and he has soft hands around the net."

"Not sure about that Terrence Day," Crawford said. "Dude's a bit slow. I'm not getting that pickup."

"Management likes its veterans," Rocket said.

"We got to run, bro," Crawford said. "Good luck tomorrow!"

Rocket gave them a thumbs-up as Rino drove away. They were the craziest fans he'd ever met. He was surprised Rino and Griff weren't wearing their tinfoil Stanley Cup hats. He bet they slept in their Racers gear.

The bus came and Rocket got on. He dozed the whole time.

As it pulled up near his apartment building, all he could think about was getting inside, having a quick snack and then taking a nap. He had to get rid of this fatigue.

He walked into the lobby.

"Get out! I do not want to see you back here," Ritchie shouted. "You are a bad person."

Rocket stopped in his tracks. Then he saw a second man leaning against the wall by the elevators.

"I go where I want," the man said, "and you'd better watch your mouth, or I'll call immigration, and you can go back to whatever jungle you came from. Minus a few teeth."

"I have the right to be here," Ritchie said. "Call the government persons, Carl. I do not care — and I am not scared of you."

Carl burst out laughing. He had short-cropped blond hair, shaved closely on the sides and back, and a nose ring and two earrings.

"'Government persons?' Learn English already," Carl said.

Rocket had heard enough. "The man asked you to leave, so here's the door." He pointed to it.

Carl laughed again. "Who's the punk?"

"You are the punk," Ritchie said. "I see you here again, I call the police. You do not like that, do you?"

The smile disappeared from Carl's face. "Best not get involved in my stuff."

"Last warning," Rocket said. "Use the door before I don't give you a choice."

Rocket recognized Carl's type from his old neighbourhood: a tough talker, but not a tough guy. That was one advantage of growing up where he had. He was pretty good at figuring out who you needed to stay away from — and who was full of it.

Rocket zeroed in on Carl, balled his fists and stepped forward.

Sure enough, Carl flashed a cocky grin, shrugged and pushed off from the wall.

"I'm done my business," he said. He stuffed his hands into the pockets of his army jacket. "You guys sure you don't want to party? I can hook you up with some good stuff, the best. I have the best prices in town. Let me know." He flicked his chin and strolled out the door.

Ritchie scowled and his eyes darkened. "Thank you, Bryan. That is a very bad man. I warned him before to stay away, but he does not listen. I will not let drugs be sold here."

"Are you sure he's a dealer?"

"One reason to leave El Salvador was to get away from people like that," Ritchie said. "Many people die in my country because of drug war and gangs, fighting over money. I hate it, and I will not let Carl push me around so he can do his *business*."

"I don't think he'll be a problem," Rocket said.

Ritchie looked out to the street. "Mariana tells me to leave it alone. But I get mad."

Rocket patted Ritchie on the back. His landlord was a real stand-up guy. "Carl's a poser, a big talker, if you ask me. He won't be back now that he knows he has to deal with both of us."

Ritchie laughed, his usual smile back in place. "You are right, Bryan. He is a little fish. In Spanish, we say he is an *agrandado*, which means he thinks he is a big person and all important, but he is nothing and no one cares about him. Come on. Let me make you lunch. Then I must go to work."

But as the rush of adrenalin from his run-in with Carl faded, all Rocket really wanted to do was sleep. Concussion or not, something was taking a lot out of him. "You know what, I think I'll just hit the hay. I'm tired from my workout," he said.

Ritchie gave him a quizzical look. "What do you mean — *hit the hay?*"

"It means go to sleep."

Ritchie shook his head. "That is a strange one. In

Spanish, we sometimes say *meterse en el sobre*, which means to get into the envelope. Funny to translate from one language to another. Hit the hay! I like it. Anyway, I will fix a sandwich for you and put it in the fridge."

"Thanks, Ritchie."

Rocket went to his bedroom and pulled the curtains.

His phone buzzed. A text from his bud, Ty: *Saw u popped in a pair last night. Awesome work. Bring it.*

He texted back: *One more home game, then 4 game road trip. Gotta bring it. No. 1 centre hurt. Might get chance for regular shift. U good?*

Rocket lay down and closed his eyes. His phone buzzed, but he was too tired to check it.

Rory was right. He couldn't afford to get hurt now. Maybe that hit took something out of him, and maybe it was a concussion. But he had to fight through it. Megan was right about one thing. He didn't have a plan B. It was hockey or nothing.

He felt himself drift off.

CHAPTER 18

Bent at the waist, with his stick across his knees, Rocket did a wide turn.

"Let's make some N–O–I–S–E!" the announcer bellowed.

The fans rose to their feet and cheered. Rocket straightened up.

"Wake up, Rockwood," he said to himself for the tenth time.

C.C. was still hurt, and it seemed likely he'd be put on the injury list. That meant Bryan "The Rocket" Rockwood would be the Racers' number-one centre tonight and on the road trip ahead. The sour look on Barker's face when Kaufman had called Rocket's name to start was an extra bonus.

Rocket set up for the opening faceoff. The puck dropped, and the Rams' centre pulled it back to his left defenceman. Rocket gave chase, scowling at himself. He hadn't even set up properly.

Get in the game, he told himself.

The Rams' defenceman banked the puck off the wall to his left winger, who chipped it into the Racers' zone before Rory rode him into the wall. The goalie trapped it behind his net. The Racers' right defenceman went back for it. Rocket curled in front of him, figuring Rory's check had held the winger up so he'd have the space. The defenceman snapped a pass. Rocket took it on his forehand and flew up the side. Goldsy hovered up near the Rams' blue line. A pass to him would be too high risk, so instead, Rocket cut into the seam between the centre and the left winger. Both converged on him, which freed Rory up.

Rocket sent a hard saucer pass to his right to Rory, then hopped to the left to avoid a crushing check from the centre.

Rory carried it over the red line, and then rang the puck up on the glass. The Rams' goalie tried to trap it, but the puck squeaked by him. Goldsy got to it at the hash marks and knocked it into the corner. Rocket fired in from the blue line on the forecheck. The right defenceman reached out to corral the puck with his forehand, his back to the play. Rocket would get a penalty if he hit him from behind, so he veered right and curled into him.

The crowd let out a roar. Rocket had knocked the guy to the ice.

Pulling the puck out from under the defenceman, Rocket backed up along the wall. Goldsy headed to the net. Rory was camped out to the right side.

Rocket almost sent it to Rory behind the net, but the Rams' right winger was cheating down low. Instead, he snapped a pass along the wall to his defenceman on the left point. Goldsy established a strong net presence in front. Rory shifted to the top of the circle. Rocket decided to go behind the net and give the point man an outlet.

The Rams' right winger charged the point. The point man opted to send the puck along the wall to Rocket, who kicked the puck to his stick and faced the play. With the sound of the crowd ringing in his ears and the Rams' defencemen unsure of what he'd do next, Rocket relished the moment. It was a chance to get creative and make a play.

He took it two steps left. The centre came at Rocket from the goalie's glove-hand side, while the left defenceman protected the post and the right defenceman battled with Goldsy in front. The wingers stayed high to take away the point shot.

That left Rory wide open.

Rocket took another half-step left. The centre reached his stick out. Rocket saucered the puck between the guy's feet to the top of the circle, then hopped back right to avoid the hit. The centre caught a piece of his shoulder, but not enough to knock him off stride.

Rory took the pass on his forehand. The Rams' left defenceman turned to face the shot. Rocket jumped to the goalie's glove side, standing behind the left defenceman, hoping for a rebound. Rory hesitated and then, with a flick of his wrists, ripped a shot along the ice to the short-side. The left defenceman dropped to the ice to block the shot, as did the goalie. The puck went into the left defenceman's shin pads. Rocket looked down.

There it was. The puck had squeaked through.

Rocket shot without looking, lowering his left hand to get the puck as high as he could.

Then he pushed off with his left skate, bent his right

knee and swung his left arm overhead. He turned to face his teammates, drifting backwards to the boards.

Magical — a first-shift goal.

Rory's arms were apart as he skated over. He wrapped them around Rocket's shoulders.

"That's what I call top shelf," he said.

Rocket's forehander had grazed the goalie's left shoulder and zipped into the top corner, short-side.

"Way to get the puck to the net," Rocket said.

His defencemen congratulated them. "Awesome puck movement, boys," one of them said. "Goalie didn't even see it."

Goldsy gave Rocket's shin pads a tap. "Good start. Let's get another." That meant a lot to Rocket. C.C. and Goldsy were pals, and Rocket had taken C.C.'s spot.

McGill called for a complete change. Five players filed onto the ice. Rocket punched gloves as he came onto the bench. Rogers moved over to give Rocket a spot.

"Nice snipe, bro," Rogers said.

Downey leaned over and punched Rocket's knee. "You and R.C. Cola have it going," he said.

Rocket's opinion of his old linemates went way up. They were still sitting, but they were team players and happy about the go-ahead goal.

"We got the jump on them, boys," Rocket said loudly. "Let's get the next one."

A wave of fatigue washed over him, and for a moment, he saw spots. Fortunately, everyone had turned to watch the game, and no one noticed him fumbling for some water. He took off his helmet and poured some of it on his head and down his neck. The cold shocked him, but it felt good and the spots went away.

He was tempted to tell Nadav. He rolled his neck a few times.

"You feeling okay?" Rogers asked him.

"Got cross-checked last game. I'm a bit stiff."

McGill slapped Rocket lightly on the shoulder. "You're playing well. Don't let up," he said.

Rocket put his helmet back on. He had a game to play.

The two teams settled into a grinding style of play for the rest of the first and the second periods. Rocket had a good chance in close on a set-up from Rory, but the goalie had stood tall and made a tremendous glove save.

Fatigue continued to be an issue, but Rocket was able to cover it up with quick shifts. Barker was the bigger problem. He wouldn't let up about Rocket's defence: "You left the zone too fast." "Support the D in our end." "Backcheck for once in your life." The chirping never stopped.

Rory told him to ignore it and play his game.

Not so easy when your every move is micro-analyzed.

Barker was never going to let up.

CHAPTER 19

"Rockwood, change it up," Kaufman barked.

Rocket hopped the boards alongside Rory and Goldsy. With 9:25 left on the clock, the Racers were up by one. Lots of time for the Rams to come back.

The faceoff was in the Racers' end. The centre was already lined up. He tended to finesse the draw, so Rocket decided to go in hard and overpower him. The linesman held the puck out. Rocket lowered his stick. At the drop, Rocket swung his right hip into the centre and swept his stick backwards.

Their helmets banged into each other. Rocket winced. The centre had fooled him and opted for a power move also. The puck lay in their feet. Rocket pushed hard and kicked at the puck. It dribbled to the side wall, and the Racers' defenceman brought it to the corner. The centre took a step back and drilled Rocket with his shoulder. Rocket tumbled to the ice.

"Interference!" Rocket yelled at the referee. He got to his knees.

His defenceman ringed the puck around the wall to Goldsy.

Two gloves pounded into Rocket's back.

"Shut up, little boy, and play the game," the centre said.

Rocket struggled to his feet. His legs felt like clay, and his skates seemed to weigh a hundred pounds each. He wanted to take a run at the guy so badly. But the Racers needed to protect that one-goal lead, and Rocket knew the golden rule of hockey: the guy who retaliates always gets the penalty.

The right defenceman pinched, and Goldsy had to retreat into the corner, protecting the puck with his big frame.

Rocket groaned and skated over to support. He figured he could dig it out and whip it around to Rory. Goldsy saw him coming and nudged the puck along the wall with his stick. Rocket slammed on the brakes, pulled the puck toward him with the tip of his blade and set off around the net.

Rory was at the half-boards. Rocket was about to pass it, but the left defenceman pinched and the pass wasn't there. The centre was standing still in front. Dead legs or not, Rocket knew it was up to him to carry it out of their zone. He ignored the pain, rounded the net on the goalie's stick side and headed up. The quick move caught the centre off guard. All he could do was reach his stick out. Rocket swung the puck to his backhand to avoid the poke check. Rory cut inside for a pass. The Rams' right defenceman moved forward to cover Rory. Rocket decided to keep it.

Suddenly, Rory went down.

"What's that?" Rocket screamed.

The defenceman had hip-checked Rory at the knees,

and Rory had fallen to the ice like a rag doll.

Rocket's tiredness disappeared. He dropped his gloves and stick and charged. He threw a right hook at the defenceman's chin and followed up with two left hooks at his ear. The defenceman staggered back. The Rams' left defenceman pulled Rocket away by the shoulders. Rocket turned and hit him with a hook to the body.

"Easy, kid," the defenceman said calmly. "This is over." He kept hold.

He was a really big guy, with a thick, heavy frame, and Rocket could feel his strength — not a guy to mess with.

"What's with the cheap shot?" Rocket fumed.

"I get ya," the defenceman said. "But it's done."

Rocket looked up. The defenceman's beard was speckled with grey, and his forehead and the area around his eyes had a few wrinkles. He also had a dark scar running down one cheek, and his front teeth were missing. Rocket tried to pull away. No point. The guy was too strong.

"We good?" the defenceman said.

"Yeah, I'm done," Rocket said, and the guy let go.

Rocket wanted to take another run at the right defenceman. Rory was still down. Hockey had a code, though. A fight was over once you agreed to stop.

Goldsy was leading Nadav to Rory. Rocket went to him.

"Sorry, bro," the right defenceman was saying to Rory. "I thought you had the puck. Honest."

"Stand back," a linesman said to him.

Rocket looked down at Rory's face and saw

something he never thought he'd see there — fear. It chilled Rocket to his core.

A hand tugged on Rocket's sweater.

"You're in the box for fighting, number 36," a linesman said.

"The guy submarined him at the knees!" Rocket said.

The linesman began to push him toward the penalty box. For one insane moment, Rocket felt like pushing back. The defenceman who'd hit Rory was being directed to the Rams' bench.

"What about that guy? He went after his knee — on purpose," Rocket said.

The linesman didn't react. He kept pushing Rocket to the penalty box.

"Total garbage call!" Rocket was shouting. "He ends a guy's career, and you give me a penalty? Stupidest call ever."

The door opened.

"What about the third man in?" Rocket screamed. "Their left defenceman practically mugged me."

He turned his back on the linesman and stormed into the box and slammed the door shut. The glass around the box shook. The referee came over and opened the door.

"You got a fighting major and an instigation penalty, and that little temper tantrum earned you a misconduct," the referee said. "You're done for the night."

Rocket leapt to his feet. "He went after Rory's knee, on purpose. May as well give the Rams a couple of goals and get it over with. You obviously want them to win!"

"Watch your mouth, rookie," the referee snarled.

He stepped closer. "I'm giving you a break because you're a kid. You question my integrity again — ever — and every ref in this league will be on you. That's a promise. So I advise you to shut it and get off the ice before I give your team a delay-of-game penalty." He skated away.

Rocket stepped back on the ice, in shock. Goldsy handed him his gloves and stick.

"Did you get a game?" Goldsy said.

"They said I was the instigator of the fight," Rocket said. "I'm gone. Did you see the hit?"

"We all did. I think R.C. Cola's really messed. I can't believe the guy hit his bad knee," Goldsy said.

Nadav was helping Rory off.

The penalties had just been posted on the scoreboard, and the Racers' fans were making their feelings felt. A chorus of boos cascaded down, and the referee was being called every name in the book. Rocket went to the bench.

"Most ridiculous call ever," Rocket heard Crawford yell.

The boys had managed to sneak down again.

"Open your eyes, ref. Takes two guys to fight," Chaz said.

Griff shook his scarf at the ref.

"Your number 36 got a major penalty for fighting, a two-minute instigator penalty and a misconduct," the referee said to McGill. "He's gone, obviously. I need a guy in the box for the fighting major and the instigator."

"Don't really see how we got three penalties and my guy is the one carried off the ice," McGill said.

The referee pointed at the Racers' end for the faceoff and skated off without answering.

Barker stomped over to the end of the bench. "Nice work, Rockwood. A 1–0 game, and you get a major, an instigator, a misconduct, and you don't even take the other guy with you. Are you an idiot?"

"Focus on the game," McGill said to Barker.

Barker grinned at McGill. "You should focus on *winning* the game."

"I don't need you to tell me that," McGill said.

"Nope, but Floyd might have something to say about it," Barker snickered.

"Meaning?" McGill said.

Barker shrugged and moved over to the middle of the bench.

McGill took a deep breath. "Beauclair, get out there for the kill."

Barker seemed strangely smug and satisfied, like he knew a big secret.

Rocket shook his head. He went to the gate and left the ice.

"Awesome fight," Crawford cheered from the railing.

"Heavyweight champion of the world — *The Rocket*," Chaz said.

Griff waved his scarf over his head.

Rocket nodded weakly and walked past them.

Short-handed for five minutes! No wonder Barker was mad. He opened the dressing-room door. Rory sat at his stall, leaning against the wall, rubbing his face with a towel.

Was that it?

Was the knee blown out?

He hoped not. He knew Rory didn't have a plan B, either.

CHAPTER 20

Rocket filled another ice bag and gave it to Nadav. Holding the ice bags in place, Nadav wrapped a Tensor bandage around them and Rory's knee. Throughout it all, Rory remained perfectly still.

"No point jumping to conclusions," Nadav said. He taped the end of the Tensor in place. "It could be nothing, a tweak."

Rory gripped a towel in his hands. "Didn't feel like a tweak, more like a pop. Two years of rehab, and I last three games because some jerk blindsides me." He pulled the ends of the towel apart, then lowered his hands. "Stupid of me. I didn't see him. I wasn't ready."

"Not your fault. It was a cheap shot," Rocket said. "I had the puck."

A muffled roar sounded from the crowd.

"You should get out there," Rory said to Rocket.

"I sort of got kicked out — an instigator, a major for fighting and a misconduct," Rocket said.

"There goes the Lady Byng," Rory said.

Rocket laughed to be polite. Rory was putting up a brave front.

The door opened, and a tall man wearing a light grey, slightly baggy suit came in. His face was round, and he had bright red cheeks.

"Hi, sorry to interrupt. I'm Harry Dickerson, GM of the Rams. I just wanted to convey some words from Ron — the guy you got tangled up with."

Rocket opened his mouth to have his say, but Dickerson lowered his head and held a hand up. "I know what you're thinking. But Ron's not that type of guy. He isn't. He wanted me to let you know he feels really bad about you getting hurt. He honestly thought you had the puck, thought your centre had passed it. Not that it helps, but he wanted you to know that."

"Yeah, well, what I saw—"

Rory cut Rocket off. "I appreciate it. Tell Ron not to worry. It was a hockey play. I should've had my head up. It happens."

"He really feels awful," Dickerson said. "That will mean a lot to him. We're all pulling for you. You've always been a class act. Hope you get back soon."

"Thanks. I guess it's back to rehab, and we'll see how it goes," Rory said.

The crowd roared again.

"I wonder what that's all about," Rory said.

"Hold on," Dickerson popped his head out the door, called to someone and then came back in. "Sorry boys, but it's 1–1. We got a goal on the power play."

Rocket's shoulders drooped, and he let his chin drop to his chest.

Dickerson said goodbye and left.

"That was classy of Ron," Rory said. "I don't think he tried to hurt me."

Rocket didn't respond. He wasn't sure that was true.

"You could tell he felt bad," Nadav said. "Ron didn't fight back against Bryan, and I've seen him play. He's no chicken. Helder didn't do anything, either."

"Who's Helder?" Rocket said.

"The guy who wrapped you up," Nadav said. "He's been in the league for twelve years, a real warrior — and a good guy. I've met him. You definitely don't want to drop the gloves with him, though. I've seen him destroy some of the toughest dudes around."

Rocket took a sip of water. It sounded like either of those two guys could have inflicted some pain on him. He got lucky. They didn't fight him because they respected Rory — not because they were afraid of some rookie named Rockwood. He took off his sweater and tossed his elbow and shoulder pads in his bag.

Rory leaned back again, his hands clutching the edge of the bench. "This is so not good. I blow this knee up again, I'm done. It won't hold up. I've always known this could happen, but I didn't really believe it would. I guess I needed to pretend everything would be okay."

The crowd reacted to something.

"I'll go check that out," Nadav said.

Rocket began to take off the rest of his equipment.

"They scored again," Nadav called out. "It's 2–1 for the Rams with 5:32 to go."

Rory said nothing. He seemed deep in thought.

Rocket grabbed a towel. "I guess I'll go shower," he said.

He let the water flow over him for a while. He

hoped they'd at least come back and tie it up. Otherwise, his five minutes in the box would have cost them the win. Rocket finished his shower and towelled off. That Helder guy had been playing in the AHL for twelve years. Did Rocket want that? Travelling on buses, long road trips, crazy coaches and just okay money? Maybe it would be fun? Didn't seem like the guys on the Racers had much fun, though. This was a job.

The NHL dream was so big, but it still seemed so far away. He was undersized, a late-round pick and a centre with a rep for being soft on defence. He'd always been able to overcome the odds. Cut from the Oakmont Huskies in minor bantam, he'd found a new team and a great coach, Coach Sonia. Then there was the junior draft — he'd been chosen in the last round and only really made the team when the GM was fired and the coach brought Rocket back.

But how much longer could he expect to beat the odds?

He heard voices coming from the dressing room. The boys were talking quietly. He went back in. Their faces told the story as clearly as any scoreboard.

A loss.

Goldsy threw his helmet onto the floor. It hit the wall and rolled back to the middle of the room. The last few players came in and sat down at their stalls, ripping their helmets off and throwing their gloves in their bags. C.C. came in last. He wore a dark blue suit with a red tie. His shoes were brightly polished.

"Tough loss, boys," C.C. said. "Battled pretty good for the most part, then kind of lost our cool at the end. We gotta win those one-goal games. Gotta."

Rocket took a deep breath. This defeat was his responsibility.

"This one's on me," Rocket said. "I thought it was a cheap shot on Rory, and I lost it. Mouthed off to the ref, and . . . I'm sorry. Won't happen again."

His apology hung in the air.

"Discipline in the third period is key, and we'll want those two points in March . . ." C.C. said slowly. "But, you're a rookie, and that was a bad hit." He looked at Rory. "How's it feel?"

Rory tapped the ice packs with his right hand. "Don't think it's a good-news story. Won't really know until tomorrow. Guess the doctors will tell me."

"That's a warrior right there, boys," C.C. said, nodding at Rory. "Let's give it up for R.C. Cola."

C.C. began clapping and everyone joined in.

"So, some more bad news," C.C. said. "Coach Mack is gone. Ray-Ray fired him after the game. I wasn't consulted so . . . There it is. Mack's a good guy, and he wants to come in to speak to us. Hang on." He opened the door.

McGill came in, ashen-faced. He looked smaller to Rocket, like he'd lost twenty pounds since the game ended.

"I just wanted to thank you for your hard work," McGill said. "It's been an honour to coach you. I'm disappointed we couldn't keep going, but management's decided to go in another direction. Anyway, lots of luck."

Then he went around the room and shook each player's hand. Rocket felt awkward. He barely knew the coach, and McGill hadn't paid him much notice.

"Thanks for giving me a chance to play," Rocket said. He didn't know what else to say in a situation like this.

"I admire what you did today," McGill said. "Good teammate. Can't let them think we'll put up with that. Tough to take the penalties, but you showed some jam. You're a real player." He gave Rocket's hand a hard squeeze and moved on.

That was nice to hear. At least his coach — or ex-coach — didn't blame him for the loss.

McGill and C.C. embraced by the door.

"This isn't right," C.C. told him.

"It's the business," McGill said.

"You'll find a spot," C.C. said. "You need me to talk to anyone, just give me a call. I'm totally on your side."

"Me, too," Goldsy said.

The rest of the guys murmured their support.

McGill seemed genuinely moved. He offered a brief smile and nodded to them. "You'll do well. There's a lot of character in this room. Take care, boys."

He left, and the next moment the door flung open and Floyd, Blywood and Barker came in.

"A joke! A total joke!" Floyd said. His eyes flashed angrily as he marched into the centre of the room.

Barker leaned against a wall, hands in his pockets, a half smile playing across his lips, almost as if he were stopping himself from laughing outright.

"Stupid penalties, lousy penalty killing, no character — this isn't going to happen to me," Floyd said. "You all sucked tonight — totally sucked."

C.C. crossed his arms and stared at the floor.

"I get we have some injuries," Floyd continued.

"Get over it, man up and play hockey like pros."

Blywood shuffled over a few steps and sat down on the edge of a stool.

"I had to let your coach go tonight," Floyd went on. "He's a good man, but the reality is *you* fired him. You gave me no choice, not after that loss. We don't take major penalties in the third period and then give up two late goals. Never. And just because I fired the coach, don't think your jobs are safe. Uh-uh. I'll do whatever it takes to win."

Floyd held an arm out to Barker. "Bottom line is McGill was too soft on you guys, way too soft. As of this moment, Coach Barker is in charge. The next change I make will be in this room, and it won't be a coach. Get me?"

Floyd thrust his chin out and eyed the players. "I'll let Coach Barker have the floor now. I'm too sick to my stomach to stay any longer."

Blywood jumped to his feet and opened the door. Floyd went out.

"About time, Ray-Ray," Rocket heard Stella cry from the hallway. "I'm hungry."

Barker pushed off from the wall with his shoulder blades. He sauntered to the middle of the room, hands still tucked in his pockets. He took a deep breath and let the air seep out.

"We are about to go on a road trip. This trip has to be about doing the little things, playing team defence, blocking shots, taking away shooting lanes. Don't get me wrong; I respect Coach Mack. I do. But things were slipping. We can't win playing like this."

He puffed out his chest and grinned.

Rocket barely listened. This wasn't happening. It couldn't. Then it got worse.

Barker walked right at him. "You do that again, Rockwood, and you'll sit on the bench so long you'll get splinters in your butt. That was selfish. I'm okay with standing up for a teammate, but mouthing off to the ref — a misconduct? That's bush-league hockey. You got me?"

Rocket nodded.

He understood all too well. Barker wanted to send him as far away from the NHL as he could.

CHAPTER 21

The bus jerked forward. Rocket bumped into the man in front of him.

"Sorry," Rocket said.

The man glared back.

Rocket turned away. He didn't need any more trouble. Practice this morning had been a nightmare. Barker was on him constantly, criticizing every move, every shot, every pass. As Rocket had left the ice, Barker had called him "a total, useless waste of space."

Now Rocket had the worst headache. He hoped Ritchie had some Aspirin, or he'd have to run to the drugstore. All he wanted to do was sleep.

Rocket glanced at his phone. Rory had a doctor's appointment in thirty minutes, then an X-ray this afternoon. He'd texted Rocket and said that the knee didn't feel too bad this morning.

C.C. was still out for the upcoming road trip. If Rory was seriously injured, the Racers would be down two key players.

Rocket left the bus and hurried along the sidewalk. He'd promised to play ball hockey with Rafa and Leona in the laneway behind the building. It was the last thing he felt like doing. Still, he could probably suck it up for half an hour. He remembered how often he'd been disappointed by his dad — always an excuse why they couldn't get together. Even though Rafa and Leona weren't Rocket's kids, he still didn't want to let them down.

He pushed the door open and stepped into the lobby.

"You are getting out right now!" Ritchie yelled. He pushed Carl in the chest.

"I have business," Carl said menacingly.

"You go. I do not want your *business* in my building," Ritchie said. He stepped closer.

"You're costing me money," Carl said. "You're going to get hurt." He pushed Ritchie away.

"You are not scaring me," Ritchie said. He pushed Carl back.

Rocket grabbed Carl from behind and whirled him toward the door. He'd taken enough abuse from Barker. He wasn't putting up with any garbage from a jerk like Carl.

"Out the door, now, or I'll call some of my teammates, and we'll explain some things to you — very clearly," Rocket said. He showed Carl the Racers crest on his sweatshirt.

A bluff, but Carl wouldn't know that.

Carl looked at Rocket's sweatshirt. "*You're* a Racer? And you live in this dump?"

"Where do you want me to live?" Rocket shot back.

Carl straightened up and smoothed his jacket out. "I got a right to do business with whoever I want. This is a free country. You can't stop me."

"I see you in this building again and you'll be seriously unhappy," Rocket said calmly.

His head was still pounding, but he forced himself to look relaxed, as if he would like nothing better than to fight.

Carl's face turned pale. "Yeah . . . Whatever. I got lots of clients. I don't need this." He reached for the door.

"Typical," Rocket muttered. He shrugged and turned to Ritchie. "The trash is gone," he said loudly.

Ritchie reached his arm out. "Look out!" he yelled.

Something — or someone — hit Rocket from behind.

He couldn't say what happened next. He tried opening his eyes, but he couldn't focus. Everything was fuzzy. His cheek felt cold. In the background, he heard some muffled talking, like someone was speaking to him underwater. His head spun and felt heavy. Something was resting on the small of his back.

"Bryan?"

His eyes slowly began to focus. The floor? He was lying on the floor?

"Bryan, do you hear me? Bryan?"

Rocket knew that voice. Who was it?

"Are you able to sit up?" That was Ritchie.

Of course, he could sit up. He tried to tell Ritchie that, but for some reason, the words didn't come out. He pushed up with his hands. His stomach lurched, like he was on a roller coaster, and for a moment, he thought he might throw up. The floor began to spin.

Ritchie helped him to sit.

"That awful Carl hit you from behind. He runs away, too, the *cobarde*."

Rocket took a deep breath. He remembered telling Carl off and turning to talk to Ritchie. He must have been sucker-punched.

"Should we take him to a doctor?" Mariana said.

"I am a doctor," Ritchie said flatly.

"I know that, Ricardo," Mariana said. "I only meant . . ."

"I am sorry. I am being a rude person. It is not you I am angry at. I forget that here I am cleaner of buildings, nothing more."

"You will always be a doctor," Mariana said.

"You're a doctor?" Rocket blurted.

Ritchie peered into Rocket's eyes and put a hand on the back of his neck. "I am a doctor in El Salvador. Here, I am not allowed to be one." He touched Rocket's back. "You have most definitely received a concussion — most definitely. That was a very bad hit to your head, and you probably received another hit from the floor. You should probably get a scan to make sure you didn't crack your skull."

Rocket struggled to understand. It was like his brain had stopped working. "Carl hit me?"

"He did," Ritchie said. "Then the coward runs away."

Their apartment door opened.

"Rocket Man!" Rafa cried. "Can we play ball hockey now?" He wore a Racers hockey jersey.

"I'm playing, too," Leona said. She paused. "Are you all right?" she asked, kneeling beside Rocket and rubbing his arm.

"What happened?" Rafa said.

"That bad man, Carl, punched Bryan from behind," Ritchie said.

"¡*Qué cobarde!*" Rafa exclaimed.

"Do you think you can stand?" Ritchie asked Rocket.

Rocket tried to summon the energy. He felt completely drained, like he'd played five hockey games in a row. Ritchie and Mariana reached under his armpits and pulled him to his feet.

"Mariana, you need to go to work," said Ritchie. "We will take him to the hospital. Children, please get your shoes — and bring something to read. We may have to wait for some time. Hospitals are slow."

"I'm leaving tomorrow — on a road trip," Rocket said to Ritchie.

Ritchie grunted. "You will be taking a hockey vacation. Concussions are very hard to judge. Maybe a few days, maybe a few weeks — or even months. You never know."

Again, Rocket struggled to understand. A few months? That was impossible.

They went outside. The sun was blazing, and Rocket had to shut his eyes. He would have fallen to the pavement if Ritchie hadn't held him tight.

The kids came running out.

"We'll play ball hockey tomorrow," Rafa said. "You rest up."

Ritchie waved his hand over his head. A taxi slowed and made a U-turn.

Rocket squeezed his eyes together and then opened them.

He could see he was in front of the building. How had he gotten here? It was all a fog.

"Where am I?" he said.

"My goodness, this is not good," Ritchie said. "You have been hit in the head, Bryan. Carl hit you. You have a concussion."

Rocket took a few moments to process that.

"Who's Carl?" Rocket said.

CHAPTER 22

Rocket took off his sunglasses and began to climb. After two stairs, he had to reach for the handrail and stop.

He'd barely managed to drag himself out of bed this morning. They'd spent half the night at the hospital to find out Ritchie was right — a concussion.

The team was meeting in a couple of hours to catch their bus for the road trip. Rocket figured it would be smarter to tell Blywood about it in person.

His headache was raging.

"Up you go, whiner," he told himself.

He made it, but it seemed to take forever. At the top of the stairs, he had to stop to regain his breath. He heard voices from Blywood's office. The door was open.

"I'll turn this team around so fast their heads will spin." Barker was in there.

Last guy he wanted to talk to. Rocket was tempted to text Blywood instead.

"C.C. down. Colbert down. Strauss flamed out. Two guys retire on me. What a season, and it's only a few games in," Floyd said. "My dad's on my case, big time. We gotta start winning."

Just get this over with, Rocket told himself, but he didn't move.

"Who do you want on the first line?' Blywood said.

"That Rockwood kid didn't look bad to me," Kaufman said.

"He's a joke," Barker said. "Allergic to his own end."

"He's got an offensive upside. We can teach him," Kaufman said.

"We have a championship team. We don't need a five-foot-tall rookie who's still learning to play the game," Barker said. "For some stupid reason Landry thinks Rockwood can learn to play defence. He can't. If it was up to me, I'd cut him now so he could go serve coffee somewhere. That's all he's good for."

"I'd cut that Turner Rogers, too," Floyd chimed in. "That kid has no character."

"He put up some big numbers in junior. Landry's pretty high on him," Kaufman said.

"With C.C. hurt, we could use some more offence," Blywood said. "Terrence Day's never been a scorer, and Beauclair can't do it all on his own. Rockwood looks like he can put the puck in the net."

"Rockwood's not the answer. Make a trade and get someone," Barker snapped.

"High-scoring centres don't just magically appear," Kaufman said.

Rocket almost smiled at this. Barker could throw all the shade he wanted, but the Racers needed centres, and without Rocket and C.C., they were seriously undermanned up the middle.

"We can't win with a midget centre," Barker said.

The room went quiet.

Rocket gathered himself and walked to the door. He knocked on the frame.

"Yeah?" Blywood said.

Rocket popped his head in. "Hi."

Barker smirked, obviously not upset that he might have been overheard. Floyd looked annoyed. Kaufman sat back in his chair, expressionless.

"Bryan texted me earlier and said he needed to talk to me," Blywood said uneasily.

"About playing some defence?" Barker shot out.

Rocket forced a chuckle. "Not that, although I know I have to get better. In my own end — in all the ends. I mean, in all the zones." He was sounding like an idiot. "Anyway, it's kind of bad news. I sort of got hurt yesterday. It may be a concussion."

All four men sat up.

"Did that happen in the fight the other night?" Barker said.

"Um, no. It was after yesterday's practice. At home, where I'm staying. There's this guy, Carl, and he hangs out at my apartment building sometimes. Bit of a bad dude. My landlord, Ritchie, thinks he's a drug dealer."

"Rockwood, we don't need a two-hour history of your life. How'd this happen?" Barker said.

Rocket flushed. He should have just texted.

"It's a bit weird — the story, I mean," Rocket said.

Barker sighed, and he leaned back, arms crossed.

"This Carl guy, he was in a fight with Ritchie," Rocket began.

"Who's Ritchie again?" Barker said.

"The landlord," Kaufman replied.

"This is like a freakin' soap opera — and about as interesting," Barker said.

Floyd laughed.

"So, why's Ritchie fighting Carl?" Barker asked Kaufman.

Kaufman pointed at Rocket. "Ask him."

Rocket's urge to bodycheck Barker into the wall was so strong it hurt — almost as much as his head. The lights were killing his eyes, but he didn't dare put his sunglasses on. He'd look too goofy.

"Carl is the drug dealer," Rocket continued, "and Ritchie told him to leave the building, and he wouldn't. So they were fighting, and then—"

"Drugs?" Barker said. "You're mixed up with a dealer?"

"No," Rocket said. "Carl is the dealer. I don't know him."

Barker looked at Floyd and shook his head dramatically.

"I pulled Carl off Ritchie and told him to leave," Rocket said. "When I had my back to him — Carl, I mean — he surprised me with a punch to my head. I guess I went down pretty hard. That's what Ritchie told me. I was at the hospital last night, and the doctor said I have a concussion. They did a CT, and fortunately I didn't crack my skull or anything. The doctor said I could've."

Barker threw his hands up. "This is awesome. Now we're down three forwards, all because this one is messing around with drug dealers. Beautiful. The papers will have fun with that."

"I know a few boys down at the *Guardian* and the

cop shop," Blywood said. "I can keep this quiet."

Floyd stomped his feet as he stood up. His chair went flying backwards. "Why do I have to deal with this garbage? I'm not paying this kid to sit on his butt. I'm paying him to play."

Blywood picked up the chair. "If he's hurt . . ."

"How bad is it?" Kaufman said to Rocket.

"The doctor said two or three weeks. Maybe more," Rocket said. "Problem is, this could be my second concussion. I took that cross-check to the neck in the Marlies game, and . . . and I was kind of groggy after that."

Barker slapped his thighs and looked around the room. "Do I hear three concussions? How about four?"

Floyd kicked the chair. It went skidding against the wall.

"We can put him on the injured reserve list and bring someone else in," Blywood said.

"I'm not paying," Floyd fumed. "I'm not made of money."

"You shouldn't have to, either," Barker said. "There's no way we can replace him for the trip, so what if we suspend him for a week without pay? We can decide what to do with him when we get back. We'll keep him on the roster and put him on the injured reserve list — just not as a concussion. That will raise too many questions. We'll say lower-body injury and leave it at that. We can talk to Landry about it when the trip's over. He's the guy who wanted Rockwood on the team."

Rocket's heart pounded. He couldn't afford to lose a day's pay, let alone a week's. He was almost out of money. And what if they cut him?

"I like the sound of that," Floyd said. "We'll call it a suspension for missing a team meeting." He thrust his face close to Rocket's and jabbed two fingers into his chest. "You keep your mouth shut. You do not want to mess with me."

"Maybe next time you'll stay out of trouble, Rockwood," Barker said. "Professional hockey players don't get in fights with drug dealers."

"I haven't been p-paid yet," Rocket stammered. They ignored him.

"I should run him out of hockey — just to prove a point," Floyd said.

"This team is so messed," Barker said. "We need a centre — any warm body will do."

"I could give Strauss a call," Blywood suggested.

"Great! We'll never win another faceoff," Barker said.

"To be fair, he's not a centre," Blywood said.

"He is a solid right winger," Kaufman put in.

"Better than nothing," Floyd muttered. "Fine. Call him."

Rocket caught Barker looking at him, his mouth twisted in a cruel smile.

Floyd was poking at his phone. Blywood shuffled papers on his desk.

Kaufman alone seemed sympathetic, but his body language made it clear there was nothing he could do.

"What should I do during the road trip?" Rocket asked.

"I don't care," Barker said. "Go hang out with Ritchie, or Carl, or whoever. We'll decide what to do with you when we get back."

"And keep your big mouth shut," Floyd said. "Your only comment is 'No comment.'"

"Yes, sir," Rocket said weakly.

Barker waved his hand toward the door. Rocket stood there, trying to come up with some sort of protest.

"That was the signal for you to go," Barker said.

Rocket backed out of the room.

Barker got up and slammed the door shut.

Rocket just stood there, staring at the door. He could hear laughing inside.

Suspended without pay? He'd just told his mom he would be sending her some money.

They'd said Landry wanted him here, so hopefully Landry would stick up for him. And as long as C.C. was out, the Racers still needed a solid centre.

He'd have to make sure he was ready to play when the team got back from the road trip. No choice. He'd tough this out and prove he belonged.

He had to be ready to play.

CHAPTER 23

Rocket moved further under the giant overhang to get away from the sun. His eyes were still really sensitive, even with sunglasses. He should have taken another painkiller. His head was throbbing.

He checked the time. Maddy's bus should be there soon.

After being suspended, he'd called his mom to tell her — leaving out a few details, like the fight and the concussion. He told her he'd missed a team meeting. It was hard to lie to her, but he didn't want her to worry.

Then, out of the blue, Maddy had called and said she was coming to visit Saturday. He couldn't talk her out of it. Hopefully, he could fake being well, and she wouldn't suspect anything. The biggest challenge would be covering up his fatigue. He could fall asleep right now.

He leaned against the bus station wall and closed his eyes.

That felt good.

"Mr. Rockwood, have you been a bad boy?"

He pushed himself off the wall. "Megan?"

She was leaning out of the passenger window of a car. "I was the last time I checked," she said with a laugh.

André leaned over from the driver's side and waved. The back window opened. Maddy stuck her head out.

"Hey, guys. Great to see you," Rocket said.

"So, just one question," Maddy said. "How exactly did you miss a team meeting? And how can they suspend you for a week, without pay, for that?"

"That's two questions," Rocket said, coming over to the car. "And it's a long story. Basically, Coach Barker has it in for me. And the owner overreacted. It'll be okay."

"What's with the mega-shades?" André said. "You don't want to be recognized on the streets?"

"Yeah, it's a pain. I can't go anywhere without getting mobbed," Rocket said. He took them off and tried not to wince.

"Get in, Superstar," Maddy said, pushing the back door open.

Rocket slid in next to her. "I thought you were taking the bus?"

She shrugged. "We thought we'd all surprise you with a visit."

"Where'd you get the sweet wheels?" Rocket asked André.

"My dad got a new car. So this one was just sitting in the driveway, and he let me take it to school. Welcome to the A-Mobile." André paused. "Okay . . . I may need to work on the name."

"So, what's this long story?" Maddy said.

"Before you start — where to?" André said.

"Um, I told the family I'm staying with that Maddy and I would be over for lunch, but I didn't know about all of you . . ."

"Can we at least see inside your place?" Megan said. "We can go out to eat somewhere."

"I guess," Rocket said. He didn't really want to spend the money, and he knew Maddy didn't, either.

He'd asked Ritchie and Mariana not to mention his concussion. He was nervous about the kids spilling the beans, though, so maybe it would be good not to hang around there.

"Where's good to eat?" André said.

"I haven't been here that long, so I'm not sure. What do you feel like?"

André and Megan began discussing what they wanted for lunch.

Rocket grew dizzy — the sun was too bright, and his friends were speaking so fast he couldn't keep up. He needed to sleep, not eat.

Honk!

A bus had pulled up behind them and blasted its horn. The sound hit Rocket's head like a dagger.

"Gotta fly, Rocket. Directions?" André said.

"Straight ahead," he managed.

Maddy was checking him out. He needed to make a joke, show her he was okay.

"So, how long you hanging around for? I'm an important guy. Got stuff to do," he said.

"Hey, did you hear me?" André said. "Do I turn here?"

Rocket's ears were ringing. The motion of the car was making him sick. He bent over, holding his head.

"Pull over," Megan said. "Bryan? What's wrong?"

Rocket put his sunglasses on. "I just need a second. Hold on."

"I can pull over at the gas station," André said.

Rocket closed his eyes and took a few deep breaths. He began to feel a bit better once the car had stopped. He groaned and sat up slowly.

"We should go to emergency," Megan said. "Get you checked out."

"I don't need a doctor," Rocket said.

"You look pale as a ghost," she argued.

"You're not yourself, bro," André said. "Might be a good idea."

Rocket sighed. "I've already been to the hospital."

"What did they say?" Maddy said.

"You guys don't have any water, do you?" Rocket said. His mouth had gone dry.

"I have an extra bottle," Megan said.

He drank it greedily. "Sorry, guys. You came all the way to see me, and I have a . . . a headache."

"What's going on?" Maddy said. "I knew from your voice on the phone there was something. You didn't miss a team meeting. Tell me."

"You got to promise not to tell Mom," he said.

"Why?"

"She'll freak out."

Maddy's eyes narrowed. "I'm about to freak out."

"I have a concussion," Rocket said.

"You take a head shot in a game?" André said.

"I did for the first one."

"The first one?" Megan said. "You've had *two* concussions?"

"Yeah. You were right. That cheap-shot cross-check in the neck probably gave me one. Then some guy sucker-punched me in the lobby of my building."

"Okay, I need the long story," Maddy said.

"How about we head to your place?" Megan said. "I think you need to lie down."

"That's not a bad idea," he said wearily. He forced his eyes open. "Head to the next light and make a left. Sorry, but the sunshine is killing me, and I have a wicked headache. I just need to sleep for a bit, a half hour, and then I'll tell you everything."

"The A-*Machine* is on the move," André said.

Rocket's stomach lurched as the car moved forward. This was getting worse. So much for faking it.

Plus, Floyd had told him to keep his mouth shut, and here he was telling them all about it.

If the truth got out, he was done for.

CHAPTER 24

Rocket put his hands on the car and leaned his head through the passenger-side window to say goodbye. He'd slept for almost five hours. At least his headache was better.

"Sorry about today, guys," he said. "You didn't come here to babysit Rafa and Leona in the park all afternoon while I slept."

"No big deal, bro," André said. "You heal up."

"Don't let them pressure you into playing," Megan said from the back seat. "Concussions are serious. I'll do some reading, and we can talk about it."

For Megan, "some reading" meant she'd be a world expert in a day or two. There would be a flood of emails on the subject soon.

"I guess I should learn a little about the subject myself," Rocket said.

Maddy hugged him through the window. "I'll call you later. And we need to tell your mom. I mean, this is too serious to keep from her, and I'm not thrilled about lying."

"I'm not thrilled they're ripping Bryan off by not

paying him," Megan said. "It's so unfair. Don't you have a players' union you can complain to?"

"Not sure that's a great idea," Rocket said. "I just need to tough this out and get playing again."

"They have to pay you," Megan said.

"Apparently not," Rocket said.

"I bet there's an agreement between the players and the owners that says—"

"Megan, I can't be messing with them right now," Rocket said. "You get a reputation for causing trouble in hockey and you're done. No one will want you. And I'm hardly in a position to argue. I can barely walk up a flight of stairs."

"They're taking advantage of you," she said.

Rocket sighed. "I don't think it's that serious. Come on, guys. Give me a little time. I could be better by next week. And Maddy, please don't tell my mom yet. I don't want to worry her for nothing."

"One week," Maddy said, holding up a finger. "Then I tell her."

"In one week, I'll be back on the ice setting the league on fire."

She gave him a wry smile. *"Bring it."*

"Please," Megan said. "Dumbest expression ever."

"I think the dumbest expression ever is 'we're going' — because you two said that about twenty minutes ago and we're still here," André said.

Maddy gave Rocket a final hug — then Megan hopped out.

"Yeah, I didn't feel like going yet, either," André said.

Megan gently put her arms around Rocket's neck.

"Please, take care of yourself," she whispered. "Don't tell us not to worry. This is so serious, it's scary."

She was always worrying about him. Sometimes it bothered him. This time it made him feel better.

"So, do some research and figure out how to fix a concussion," Rocket said. "Shouldn't take you more than a day or two."

"I'll take the week," she said. "I want to get it right."

"Don't worry about me," André called. "I'll be fine driving back to school at two in the morning."

"Taxi!" Megan said, waving her hand over her head.

"Where to, ma'am?" André said.

She got in the car. "Just drive."

André started the car, and Maddy waved at Rocket.

Megan looked back out at him and said, "At the very least, get some less goofy sunglasses."

"I think they make me look like a rock star," he said.

"You might want to watch some videos for tips on what a rock star looks like," Maddy said.

"Be chill, bro," André called as the car drove off.

Rocket waved and then let his arm fall to his side. Nice to have friends who cared.

His phone buzzed. Megan had probably already invented a new treatment for concussions. He swiped the screen.

It was Rory. *Hey, if ur not doing anything, come by and watch some video with me.*

Rocket figured he wasn't ready to go back to bed yet, so he texted, *Ok. Be there in 20.*

It ended up taking closer to an hour. He had to take

two buses, and then it was a bit of a walk from the stop. He was tired, but his head wasn't aching so much, more like a soft pulse. The nap had definitely taken the edge off.

Rocket knocked on the door and stood back a bit to look at the place. It was a narrow two-storey row house. The door opened slowly.

"You must be Bryan," a woman said. She held a baby on her hip.

"Um, sorry . . . Is Rory around?" He checked the number. "This is 32, right?"

She laughed. "I'm Melissa, Rory's wife, and this is Angela."

Rocket squeezed Angela's little foot. "You're very cute, Angela. Do you play hockey?"

"No doubt Rory will have her in skates soon enough," Melissa said, laughing again. "We came to spend some time with him while the team is on the road. The house is empty, so I thought, why not? Nice to get the family time."

She patted Rocket's arm as he came in. "Rory told me what happened," she said. "Thanks for stepping up for him. He says the guy didn't mean it, but Rory always thinks the best of people."

"Hard to tell," Rocket said. "He apologized after. I kind of lost it. I might've cost the team the game."

He followed Melissa into the living room. The house smelled a bit like wet towels, and the carpet was dingy and grey. It wasn't hard to believe a bunch of young hockey players lived here.

"Welcome to the palace," Rory said. He tossed his ice pack aside and got up from the couch to shake hands. He gave Rocket a searching look. "You're moving a bit slow. You get dinged in that fight?"

"Not really. Just tired. How are you feeling?"

"Good news! Nothing more than a hyperextension. The doctor was surprised it wasn't worse, actually. The ligaments have healed well and the muscles around the knee are strong. I should be back skating in a few days."

Rory sat back down and motioned Rocket to a chair. "But what about you? What's the deal with the suspension? I asked C.C., and he told me you missed a team meeting. I don't remember you missing a team meeting."

"I was—" Rocket began laughing. Melissa and the baby had sat down beside Rory, and Angela was blowing air through her lips, making a raspberry sound.

Rory laughed, too. Then he looked back at Rocket. "Whatever it is, the guys aren't buying it. What really went down? And what's with the crazy shades?"

Megan was right: Rocket really did need to get new glasses. These ones were like a giant billboard that said, *I just had a concussion.*

"Can you keep this to yourself? Seriously, Floyd and Barker will kill me if they find out I told you."

"We're teammates," Rory said. "I'm not running to tell those two jerks anything."

He told Rory and Melissa the story. Rory's expression grew grim.

"They can't do that," Rory said angrily. "They have to pay you. And why the suspension?"

Rocket shrugged. "They said I was hanging around drug dealers and that would hurt the team's reputation. Floyd made me promise to keep it quiet, and Barker said

I won't get paid until after the road trip."

"Man, we both got to get healthy," Rory said.

He reached out and took Angela. She patted her dad's cheeks and blew some more raspberries. He blew a few back. "You able to watch some video?"

"I can watch a little," Rocket said. "Doctor said not too much screen time."

"We'll have a quick session," Rory said.

"Hooray," Melissa said. She didn't sound happy. "Give me Angela. I have to give her a bath. Someone I know didn't give her one, even though he promised. Nice to meet you, Bryan. Sorry about what happened. How long did the doctors say you'd be out?"

"They weren't sure. Concussions are like that. But I'm hoping to be back by the time the team returns. That's the plan, anyway."

Rory didn't look convinced.

"I hope so," Melissa said.

She went to the stairs. Rory waited until she was up on the second floor.

"She doesn't get it," Rory said. "I don't want to watch game video for hours or live in a dump like this. I want my family to have a beautiful place — and I'd much rather play with Angela and eat a bag of chips. But that won't get me back to the big leagues. I got to do it for them, to give them a future."

"Won't they have a future, even if you don't play hockey?" Rocket said. The words surprised even him. Why had he asked that?

"I guess," Rory said uneasily, "but you know what I mean." He pointed at the TV. "Have a seat. I want to show you something."

Rocket sat on the couch. A spring poked him in the back, and he moved over.

Rory started the video. It was the first period of the Rams game.

"Puck's in the right corner," Rory began. "You're in the high slot. That's not right. You got to be closer to the faceoff dot to cut off the passing lane, and you want to have your stick on your forehand to keep the puck from getting in close to the net. That also gets you closer to the corner so you can help the D if they have trouble getting control of the puck. And you'll still be in position as an outlet for a breakout."

"I figured the defenceman had him, and I would be ready for a pass up high," Rocket said.

"Watch what happens next," Rory said.

He let the play run. The winger threw the puck behind the net. The Racers' right defenceman reached for it, but it hopped over his stick and continued to the other winger at the hash marks. The Rams' centre skated down low and took a pass in the slot, cut left and sent a backhander, short-side. The goalie knocked it away with his blocker.

"I remember that play," Rocket said. "Bad luck. It hopped over our D-man's stick. And no chance he scores on a backhand from there."

"You have to be in position to handle the worst-case scenario, not the best," Rory said. "The centre got a pass in your zone. You have to be there, regardless of what you think will happen. Anticipation is fine, but you have to at least be in the area. If he'd been a right-handed shot, it would've been a serious scoring chance. Are you up for more?"

Rocket's head was spinning a bit, but he said, "I think so."

Rory fast-forwarded to another play. "Puck's dumped into our end. You're not on your man."

He ran the play. The Rams' centre roared in and plastered the Racers' defenceman against the boards. The Rams' winger got the loose puck and began a cycle down low.

"You got to get a piece of your guy in the neutral zone, or at least get in his way — not obstruction because that's an easy penalty call — but something to slow him up. You let him go, and they got possession."

They watched another play. Rory pointed out Rocket's bad positioning and wrong stick placement.

"I guess Barker's right," Rocket said. He was thoroughly depressed.

"Don't say that," Rory said. "You're a great player, and I think if you work on this, you'll move up. Barker's going to be a huge problem for all of us, but especially you. Maybe he's still holding a grudge, but I also think he's the type that likes picking on people. He obviously has it in for you. Might be worth getting your release and trying to play for someone else."

"Like who? I'll be out of the league."

"East Coast, Europe, Russia? Then you come back when you've put up some solid stats."

"I don't want to sound bitter, but that would totally suck," Rocket said.

They turned back to the TV as the next play started. Rocket felt sick to his stomach. It was obvious that he defended as an afterthought and was constantly looking to attack, even if the puck was deep in the Racers' end.

Barker and Landry were right, and the thought left a very bitter taste in his mouth.

CHAPTER 25

Rocket tiptoed as quietly as he could to the living room. He'd slept practically the entire day. Now it was midnight, and he couldn't sleep.

His life had become a blur — he slept all the time. The Racers had come back from their road trip a week ago, and he could still barely stay awake for more than a few hours at a time. Hockey seemed a distant memory.

Other than a dinner invitation and a few texts from Rory, and one text from C.C., Rocket hadn't heard from the other Racers. The guys had obviously forgotten him.

He plunked himself on the couch and opened his laptop. He could tolerate the screen for half an hour, a few times a day.

Rocket spent the time reviewing hockey videos of himself and others, including NHL players. He'd also begun taking detailed notes. He was learning more and more, like how a slight change in stick position can shut down a power play or take away a pass to the slot.

The hardest part of it was that he didn't make one

major mistake over and over. The mistakes were subtler: errors in judgment, getting to the boards a step late, leaving the zone too soon, failing to block a passing lane. Rory told him not to sweat it; Rocket needed to go through the learning process like everyone else.

Rory had taught him something else. Pros study the game — constantly.

Rocket began reviewing a video of the Racers' last game. They'd won 4–2. Rory had told Rocket to watch C.C.

"Nice," Rocket said as C.C. beat the opposing centre to the top of the circle in the Racers' end.

As the video went on, Rocket jotted down notes and kept up a running commentary.

"Get in the passing lane."

"Watch the slot."

"Lift his stick."

He rewound the video to see C.C.'s spacing. The Racers' captain knew what he was doing. Rocket stared at the screen. How could a player that good not be in the NHL?

He flipped to another video and found one of his own shifts. Rogers passed to him in the neutral zone, then —

A bedroom door creaked open. Rocket looked up.

Rafa beamed a smile and stepped out.

"You should be in bed," Rocket said.

"Can't sleep. Why are you up?"

"Same, I guess."

"What are you doing?"

"Watching myself play hockey."

"Why?"

"To learn how to play better."

"You already know how to play."

"You can always improve, Rafa."

Rafa slid onto the couch.

Rocket laughed and ruffled his hair. "You want to watch a little?"

"Sure."

"They have the puck in our corner," Rocket said. "I'm supposed to cover the centre in the high slot, and if we get the puck, I have to—"

"This is boring," Rafa said. "Can we play a game?"

"Well, maybe you should try to sleep."

"Come on. One game."

"What do you want to play?"

"I don't know."

Rocket closed the laptop. "A quick game of crazy eights?"

Rafa nodded vigorously.

"Can you get the cards?" Rocket said.

Rafa dashed to a desk tucked into a nook and opened a drawer. He dug around until he found the cards.

Rocket shuffled and dealt them.

"I want to play," Leona said. She scampered onto the couch.

"Do you guys ever sleep?" Rocket said. These two didn't have an off switch.

"I don't need to sleep," Leona said.

"Liar. You sleep all the time," Rafa said.

"You do, too," Leona said.

"Let's move to the floor. There's more room," Rocket said. He dealt Leona a hand. "Remember the rule," he said dramatically. "No tears when I win."

That was his go-to joke whenever they played a game. It always got a reaction.

"You haven't won yet," Leona said.

"I don't cry," Rafa said.

"You cry all the time," Leona said. "You cried yesterday."

"Did not."

"Did, too."

"Okay, guys," Rocket said. "Not important. I was joking. Nobody is going to cry. Now, who goes first?"

"Me!" they cried together.

"I'll go," Rocket said. "You'd both be good hockey players. You're competitive."

"What does that mean?" Leona said.

"You like to win," Rocket said.

"No tears." Leona grinned as she put a ten of hearts on top of his ten of diamonds.

Mariana came out of her bedroom. "Children, you need to let Bryan sleep — and it's late for both of you."

"I can't sleep, Mamá," Rafa said.

"Me, neither," Leona said.

She sounded so sad, Rocket and Mariana cracked up.

"Why are you laughing?" she demanded.

"No reason, Leona," Mariana said.

"We have to finish," Rafa said. "Rocket says it's bad luck to start a game and not finish."

Mariana gave Rocket a sideways glance.

Rocket smiled. "I kind of did. Besides, I slept so much today that I'm wide awake."

"How are you feeling?" Mariana said. The entire family had been incredibly kind to him while he dealt with his concussion.

"I feel pretty good right now. It's weird. It comes and goes. Some moments I think I'm ready to hit the ice, and a minute later, I have to lie down."

Mariana sat next to Rafa. "We can play one game," she said. "But deal me in."

The front door opened. Ritchie, his hair a bit messy and his eyes bleary, offered them a tired smile.

"Papá!" Rafa and Leona cried. They jumped up and ran over for a hug.

"You are so late tonight, Ricardo," Mariana said.

Ritchie kissed and hugged his kids. "The boss must like me. He wants me to stay and work for a long time. Too bad he does not like to pay me for it." He laughed.

"He has to pay you for your work," Rocket said. Ironic for him to say that: the Racers had only now started to pay him again.

"He pays me my wage," Ritchie said, "but he has a problem with paying me overtime."

Mariana rose to give her husband a hug. "He is breaking the law. You work too many hours and do not get paid what you should."

Ritchie embraced his wife, then said, "I will definitely tell my boss. I am sure he will change his mind. But for now, I am happy to have the work and to earn the money I do. Now, why are *los pequeños* still awake? Explain yourselves."

"We can't sleep. We're playing a game of crazy eights. Come here, Papá," Rafa said, patting the floor. "You can sit next to me."

Rocket dealt out another hand.

"No tears when *I* win, Papá," Rafa said.

"There will be many tears when I win," Ritchie said,

sitting down. He looked at his cards and put the queen of spades down. "A-ha! Pick up five."

"No, Papá. You go after Mamá," Leona cried.

"And you can't put a spade on a heart," Rafa said.

"Oh, I am so foolish." Ritchie winked at Rocket and picked up the card.

Ritchie continued to clown around. Soon, he had everyone laughing. Rocket sometimes wondered how Ritchie kept his spirits up and was so positive about life. Here was a doctor who had to clean buildings all day, who was ripped off by his boss and who was trying to adjust to life in a foreign country. He seemed to have so little, but he still gave so much.

Rocket suddenly felt terribly sad. He'd never had a family like this. His parents had divorced when he was little. He hadn't seen his dad much since then. His mom had to work a lot to make ends meet, and Rocket had spent a lot of time alone. It got better when Maddy moved in, but Rocket hadn't really lived at home since he was drafted as a junior. Maybe that's why he loved playing hockey so much. He never felt lonely on the ice.

"Your turn, Rocket Man," Rafa said.

Rocket threw an eight on the pile. "Make it diamonds."

"You shouldn't waste your eights so early," Leona scolded.

She was an interesting kid, feisty and demanding, but also the first to cheer her family on and always ready with a hug. Rafa acted like a tough kid, but deep down, he was sensitive and kind. Their parents obviously adored them both.

Rocket thought of Rory, then. His friend was so

obsessed with getting back to the NHL, he was missing out on time with Melissa and Angela.

Was it possible to have both — a family and a hockey career? Rocket wondered about his future. Could he have it all? And if not, what was more important?

"Rocket," Leona said. "It's your turn again. You're being such an empty head."

"Sorry. I was trying to decide which awesome card to play."

Leona played next and then Mariana.

"Pick up two," Mariana said to Ritchie.

"I will not forget this betrayal," Ritchie said.

Rafa and Leona giggled.

Rocket shifted to get more comfortable.

"I think Bryan is getting tired," Mariana said.

"Okay," Leona said instantly.

"No, no. I'm good. Let's finish. Besides, I want to see Rafa cry."

"Oh, yeah, look at this." Rafa put down three sixes. He knocked on the floor twice. "One card left," he said proudly.

"Are your friends coming back to see you soon, Bryan?" Ritchie asked.

Rocket picked a card from the pile. "I'm not sure. They go to different schools, so they have to figure out a time that works for all of them."

"They are nice kids," Mariana said. "They worry about you."

"They do," Rocket said. "I just need to get healthy and start playing again — and get into the NHL. Then I can worry about them."

"When will you be healthy?" Leona said.

"Soon," Rocket said.

Mariana cast a worried glance his way. "Do not rush back. Make sure you feel one hundred percent healthy."

"Pick up two," Ritchie said gleefully.

"Ugh," Rafa groaned. He reached for the cards.

Rocket looked over at his computer. Tomorrow he'd pick those online courses and sign up for the winter term. Megan was right. His family needed him to have a plan B. It was selfish not to. Despite all of his hard work, hockey might not be in his future. And if that happened, he'd never be able to help his mom and Maddy.

"I win!" Leona squealed, her arms over her head. "Everyone has to start crying."

"One more game?" Rafa pleaded. "I almost won."

"It's late, and Bryan needs his sleep to heal," Mariana said.

Actually, this was the best Rocket had felt in weeks. Time spent like this would help him heal faster than sleeping or watching hockey videos. He collected the cards.

"One more — if that's okay with you, Mariana?" Rocket said. "But I'm actually trying this time. And absolutely no tears when I am the champion."

The two kids howled in protest as Rocket dealt the cards.

CHAPTER 26

Rocket forced himself to jump down the last two stairs. He had to see if it hurt.

It did, a bit, but he didn't want to think about it. He needed to start working out.

He was so bored. After four weeks of watching Racers games from the press box, he wanted some action. He'd also watched countless hours of hockey videos, taken endless notes and asked Rory and Kaufman a million questions — all the while suffering a nonstop barrage of insults from Barker. He'd even started calling Rocket "Head Case." The guys on the team hadn't picked up on it, but Rocket worried that it was a matter of time before they made the connection to his injury.

It was difficult to say that the Racers actually missed him. They were playing over .500 hockey and were coming off three straight wins. Strauss was doing well. He could downright play, although he still struggled in the faceoff circle. Terrence Day worked hard, but his footspeed was an issue.

Barker was quoted in the newspaper as saying that

the Racers were winning because of discipline and toughness — in other words, because of their new head coach. Rocket thought Rory and C.C.'s return to the lineup was the real reason. Along with Goldsy, their line was scoring a ton.

His phone buzzed. It was Maddy. *How are u doing?*

He texted back, *Working out as we speak. Hope 2 be back soon.*

Maddy's response was immediate. *Great. Don't rush it. You have 2 heal. We're fine.*

She was still so worried about him. So were Megan and his mom. They were almost constantly in touch. He wished he could give them good news.

What's new with U? he asked.

Got a new part-time job. Pays well, lots of hours, she texted.

How was she going to handle that and keep her grades up? *Hope not 2 many,* he answered.

Just the right amount. Now, get back 2 your workout, slacker!

He closed his eyes and took a deep breath. Worrying about Maddy wasn't going to get him anywhere.

"*Yo, yo, yo,* the Rocket is in the house," Rory said as Rocket entered the workout room.

Rocket nodded, then took his sweatshirt off and tossed it on a table.

"You ready to do some exercise, or are you going to whine about some itsy-bitsy concussion?" Rory said, laughing.

"A little whining, probably, but I'm ready to go hard at it."

Rory popped a pill in his mouth and took a sip of

water. "Just a little something to dull the pain."

"How's the knee lately?" Rocket said.

"Ehh, not great. It hurts," Rory said. "Nadav's been giving me a shot before games. It's legal, so I'm not worried about that. I just wish the stupid pain would go away. Anyway, how about a super-intense ten-minute bike ride to start?"

Rocket flashed a thumbs-up and hopped on a bike.

"I thought I heard some voices in here," Kaufman said as he walked in. "How are you boys doing?"

"Awesome, Coach," Rocket said.

Kaufman's eyes narrowed. "I hope you're not rushing it, Bryan. Have you spoken to a doctor?"

"Not recently . . . Nadav and I meet most days, and I'm doing some workouts he designed. The doctor basically said it was up to me. I really am feeling a lot better." The words rushed out, and he began pedalling faster to prove them.

"I'll let management know," Kaufman said. "I'd like to see you out there. We need your speed and scoring."

"I want to play, more than anything. I think I'm close," Rocket said. "Like I said, I'm awesome, Coach. Ready to hit the ice."

He'd been spending more and more time with Kaufman lately. He was incredibly knowledgeable about the game. Funny how Rocket had spent his life playing hockey, including four years in major junior, and he still had so much to learn.

"Let me know how you feel after this workout," Kaufman said. "If you're good, then we'll talk about you joining us for a practice."

"Not to put you on the spot," Rory said, "but what about Strauss and Day? Would Rocket take over one of their lines?"

"I imagine a decision will have to be made," Kaufman said. "And as you can imagine, it's not my call." He patted the handlebars of Rocket's bike. "Have a good workout, boys. It would be nice to see a few others in here with you."

"C.C. and Goldsy were here yesterday," Rory said.

Kaufman nodded. He seemed distracted, as if thinking about something else.

"Interesting," he said. He tapped the handlebars again and left.

Rory was grinning.

"What?" Rocket said.

Rory raised his eyebrows. "'I'm awesome, Coach?'"

"Ugh, I know." Rocket laughed. "I wish I could take it back — along with everything else that's happened here."

Rory stood up on the pedals and began sprinting. "Pick it up, buttercup," he said.

Rocket tried to join him, but suddenly he felt exhausted, and his eyes went blurry.

"The hard times make the good times that much sweeter," Rory said. "I didn't appreciate the privilege of playing in the NHL. Took it for granted. Next time, I'll enjoy every second."

Rocket slowed down, breathing heavily. "Do you ever worry about being away from Melissa and Angela so much?"

Rory went even faster. "Yeah, of course. That's the price you got to pay. Some guys have the easy path.

Guys like us have to outwork everyone to get our shot: one shift — one workout — at a time."

Rocket turned down the tension on the bike and slowed even more.

Rory saw things in black-and-white terms. He'd do whatever it took to make it to the NHL. Every sacrifice was worth it.

Rocket wasn't sure he felt the same anymore. He used to feel so strong, almost invincible. He sure didn't feel that way now. He'd been off the ice for weeks. He also knew that one more bad hit could really mess him up. He pictured himself in his mom's apartment, sitting in front of the TV, being spoon-fed by Maddy. He couldn't do that to his family.

His time with Ritchie and Mariana had also taught him the real meaning of sacrifice. They'd left El Salvador so that Rafa and Leona could have a better life. They weren't thinking about themselves. Ritchie had given up being a doctor to come here, and he and Mariana both worked hard as cleaners.

Was Rocket playing hockey to help his family, or was it for the glory — so he could be a big-shot professional athlete?

"Pick up the pace, Rocket Man," Rory said.

There was about a thousand guys in the AHL — how many of them would finish their careers in the NHL? Would Rory? And look at C.C. He was awesome and he still couldn't break in full-time. Could Rocket really expect to do better?

He increased the tension and tried to pedal harder. He couldn't. It was like he could feel the beating of his heart in his head. He had to stop.

"I'm so out of shape," Rocket said. "Maybe I'll just do some stretching today."

"No worries, bro," Rory said. He kept going hard on the bike. "Welcome to professional hockey. In the end, it's about who can block out the pain and keep going. Wait until you play eighty-two games, then hit the playoffs. Your body never gets a chance to heal. Even those nicks and bruises add up. The ache in your body never goes away. You just push through it — and get that puck."

Was Rory right? Was it about pushing through the pain?

At this point, Rocket knew that could just make things worse.

Megan had sent him a steady stream of information about concussions. Some guys suffered headaches and dizzy spells for years. Worse, multiple concussions could cause permanent brain damage and mental problems. He'd known all that, of course. He'd just ignored it. How can you play hard when you're worrying about getting hurt?

Rocket thought of André. He'd given up playing hockey because he didn't think it was worth it. So had Ty and Adam.

At what point it would stop being worth it for him? Should he risk another injury? Was it time to go home, get a job and help his family? Or, should he go to university so he had more options later? What was the right choice?

He felt dizzy, and his legs were weak. He took a few steps to the mat area and flopped to the ground. Lying on his back, he brought his knees to his chest, as if he were stretching. Truth was he needed to lie down.

That's when it really hit him — full force. He couldn't even ride a bike for five minutes. What if he never got better?

He might already be out of options.

CHAPTER 27

Nadav held out a fist as Rocket walked into the empty dressing room.

Rocket gave it a punch.

"I heard from Kaufman you did some biking," Nadav said.

"Yeah, two days ago. Nothing major," Rocket said.

"How'd it go?"

Rocket frowned. He knew he could trust Nadav. "Not so great. I had to stop after a few minutes, but after that I was okay the rest of the day. As long as I don't push it, I feel good."

"That's a definite first step," Nadav said. "Typically, you'll start improving more and more over the next few weeks. I bet by Christmas, you'll be ready for a game."

"Christmas?" That was weeks away.

"Impossible to know for sure, but based on your progress, that's a reasonable guess."

"You're bringing me down. Any good news?"

"At yesterday's practice, Barker got hit in the ankle with a puck. He's limping."

"Sorry I missed it — even sorrier I didn't shoot it."

Nadav looked at his watch. "They'll be coming in from the pre-game skate. I have to get to work." He grabbed a bunch of towels.

"Let me help," Rocket said. He took some more towels and began placing them in front of each stall.

The door opened. Barker, Floyd and Blywood walked in.

"Head Case is finally making himself useful," Barker said.

Floyd laughed. Rocket's cheeks burned as he finished handing out the rest of the towels.

The door opened again, and Kaufman came in. He looked very serious.

"A bit of bad news," he said. "Straussy pulled his hamstring during the pre-game skate. Not sure he can go on tonight."

"What the hell?" Barker yelled. "I've had it with that stiff. Now it's a freaking hammy? Blywood, when are you going to make that trade already? We need another centre."

Blywood looked around the room nervously. "We're getting close. Teams are asking for a bit much, plus we have to get Landry on board."

"All I get is excuses," Barker said.

Blywood sat on a stool and looked down at the floor.

"What about him?" Floyd said, pointing at Rocket.

"Yeah, what about you, Head Case?" Barker said. "You going to actually play this year?"

Rocket wanted nothing more than to play — he just wasn't ready.

"I wouldn't recommend that Rocket play yet,"

Nadav said. "He still has some dizziness and—"

"Thanks for the expert medical opinion, doctor," Barker snapped. "He looks healthy enough to me and has for a couple of weeks. It's been like, what, over a month?"

"Concussions take time," Nadav said.

"Kid's made of glass, more like it," Barker said. "Hey, Head Case. You gonna step up or wuss out?"

Rocket clenched his fists to control his anger. "I obviously want to play, Coach Barker. For sure, that's why I'm here. But it's not like rehabbing a knee. I can't just work out or take medicine. It's hard to explain, but I'm sensitive to light, and I still get a headache if I push things. Even walking too fast can do it. And I'm always tired, no energy. But I'm getting better and—"

"I've been working with Bryan, along with Nadav, and I can vouch that he's putting in the effort," Kaufman said.

Barker ignored him. "I'm asking you to suck it up and be a hockey player, Rockwood."

Rocket forced himself to take a deep breath. "I just don't think I can play."

Floyd stepped forward. "Kid, you already forced us to suspend you once. Are you refusing to play? Because I don't see anything wrong with you."

Nadav cleared his throat. "With respect, Mr. Floyd—"

"With respect, shut up and finish handing out the towels, or whatever else you do around here," Floyd fumed.

"What's it going to be?" Barker said to Rocket. "We need a centre. Tonight. You ready to be a hockey player?

You ready to step up and be a man? Because if you aren't, we'll get someone who is."

Rocket took a deep breath. He was dying to get back on the ice. No one loved hockey more than he did. No one. Should he risk it? He could go out there, step up for the team and just hope he'd be okay. Not that Barker would ever thank him for it. But at least he wouldn't get suspended, or hurt his reputation.

But hockey was a contact sport. He'd definitely get hit. And that could be the end of everything.

"I'm sorry, Coach Barker, Mr. Floyd," he said. "I don't think I can play."

Barker's lips curled into a strange smile, as if he'd won something. But before Barker could react, C.C. pushed the door open and led his teammates into the dressing room.

"Good energy out there, Racers," C.C. said. He tossed his gloves into his bag and took off his helmet.

"I've got two goals in me, boys. I can feel it," Goldsy said, plopping down next to C.C. "Who else is going to pop one in — or should I just get four goals in the first period and lock it up?"

"Let's keep it close for the first period and then bust it wide open," Rory said.

Rocket stepped aside to let the guys get to their stalls.

"Settle down. Settle down," Barker said. The guys quieted. "Strauss, what's the deal?"

Strauss grimaced, and he began to rub the back of his right thigh. "It's my stupid hamstring again. I felt something go snap in the warm-up, and I can feel it tightening up. I think I need to rehab it a bit. I've been battling it since training camp. I guess I pushed it too hard."

Barker made a sour face. "You definitely push it. That I agree with."

Strauss's face went pale.

Turning back to Rocket, Barker said, "So, Head Case, you're refusing to play, even though the team needs you?"

All eyes were on Rocket now.

"Isn't he still injured? He needs to be cleared by a doctor," Rory said.

Barker's lips pressed together, and he crossed his arms. "I appreciate you played in the NHL, Colbert. But *you* need to appreciate that you're not in the NHL right now. You're here, on the Pinewood Racers, so maybe you should let management handle things. We believe Rockwood can play. He appears unwilling to do so. That's unacceptable."

"I want to play, and I will," Rocket said. "I just get a little dizzy still, and I don't have—"

"Not the whining again," Barker said, rolling his eyes.

The room was dead silent.

"You know what, Rockwood?" Floyd said. "You can leave. This room is for hockey players. You're suspended as of this moment for refusing to play. I'll deal with you after the game."

Rocket remained frozen in place. Whether it was the concussion or the humiliation, his mind wouldn't process what was happening. Maybe he should play and risk it?

"Mr. Floyd, I . . . I guess maybe I could try. I'm not trying to be difficult. It's just—"

"Get out," Floyd bellowed.

Rocket looked around the room. He could tell that his teammates were angry. They were on his side. But there was nothing they could do. Floyd and Barker controlled their careers.

"You heard the man," Barker said, nodding toward the door.

Rocket lifted his chin. He wasn't going to give Barker the pleasure of seeing him break down. Rocket walked out in a daze.

What had just happened?

CHAPTER 28

Rocket leaned against the wall and stared at the concession stand. The crowd let out a roar. He didn't bother to go into the rink to check it out. He was honestly more interested in the smell of the french fries right now.

He'd forced himself to watch the first period, then he couldn't take it and headed to the lobby. Last time he'd checked, there was about ten minutes left in the game. Racers were behind by one. Rory had knocked in a rebound to give them the early lead, but then they gave up two power-play goals in the second.

Rocket wasn't even sure why he was hanging around. It seemed likely Floyd was going to release him, whether he stayed or not.

It felt like a lifetime had passed since he'd left the dressing room. At first, he'd felt numb with shock, but that had quickly changed to anger and then, just as quickly, to fear. What would he do? He'd spent most of his life dreaming of playing in the NHL.

But so had thousands of boys.

Maybe it was time to accept that he wasn't special.

He was just a kid who'd had a good time playing hock-ey, and now it looked like that journey was over. No point feeling sorry for himself. Bad luck to get a concussion off the ice, but it happened.

He would go home and get a job — any job — to help out his family. Then Maddy could quit working and focus on school. She was super-smart, and she had what it took to be a great doctor. Rocket had to stop thinking about himself. He wasn't going to get a big, fat NHL contract.

A familiar high-pitched voice interrupted his thoughts. "Ray-Ray, all we do is hang out in this smelly rink."

Stella was walking through the lobby, Floyd beside her, his hands in his pockets, head down.

"Do I look like I like eating chicken wings and nachos?" she continued. "I don't think so. Hockey is the worst."

"Yeah, well, it helps pay for your fancy clothes and fancy dinners," Floyd said.

"I gave up my singing career for this! You told me we would be living in a big city; instead we're stuck in Pinewood."

"My dad can't live forever," Floyd snapped. "When I inherit—" He looked up, saw Rocket standing by the wall and stopped.

"Aren't you on the team?" Stella asked Rocket. "How come you're not playing? Are you hurt?"

"I have a concussion," Rocket said.

Floyd didn't react.

"There you are, Bryan," Blywood said, hurrying over. "Glad to find you. I was looking in the stands for you. I thought you'd be watching. The game's still close, but it's been tough with only three centres . . ."

Rocket just looked at him.

"Anyway, what I wanted to talk to you about . . ." Blywood stopped again. "I mean, what I wanted to say, was that, as you know hockey is a business. A very competitive one. And a hockey team can never stop trying to get better. Isn't that right, Raymond?"

"Yeah," Floyd said flatly. Rocket wished they'd all go away. He wanted those french fries.

"Yes, so, we were offered something tonight: a trade," Blywood said. "Actually, I've been talking to a bunch of teams for a few weeks, and things have gone back and forth, like they often do. We're talking to teams all the time, Bryan, to be honest. Anyway, a certain team, the Giants, wanted certain players that we were . . . uncomfortable giving up. Then, just tonight, actually about fifteen minutes ago, we struck a deal. Have to clear it with Coach Landry and the GM . . ."

"The deal is done," Floyd said harshly. "I'll handle them."

"Yes, in any event—" Blywood said.

"Just tell him, already," Floyd said.

"Right. I'll get to the point," Blywood continued. "Like I said, Bryan, hockey is a business—"

"You're the slowest talker in the world!" Floyd burst out. "We traded you to the Tennison Giants."

"Traded who?" Stella said.

"Me," Rocket said.

"Why?" she said.

"We got an unbelievable deal, that's why," Floyd said. "We're getting Steve Bannister. First, they asked for Rory Colbert, then Beauclair and a draft pick. I got involved and made the deal. We traded this kid, Strauss and Turner Rogers for Bannister. Total steal. I got a solid centre to back up C.C. and Beauclair, and all it cost me was some fourth liners."

"Your daughter will be upset that you traded Turner," Stella said. She turned to Rocket. "She dated Turner last season. Pretty sweet on him, too. But they broke up. She took it kind of hard, poor girl. I told her Turner is too young, and he's not ready to settle down. But she fell in love, and—"

"That's over with. She's better off without him. Kid can't be trusted," Floyd said. "Now, let's drop it. No one cares."

Stella smoothed her hair with her hand. "I'm sorry you got traded," she said to Rocket. "You seem like a nice boy."

The buzzer sounded.

"I should go check the score," Blywood said, heading back to the rink.

"Good luck with your new team," Stella said to Rocket.

"Thanks," he said.

"You head on up to the lounge, Stella," Floyd said. "I'll be there in a minute."

Once Stella was out of earshot, Floyd grasped Rocket by the arm. "When you get to the Giants tell them you feel sick and don't know what's wrong. Got it? Not a word about the concussion. Say you don't know how it happened — or better yet, tell them you got hit in practice yesterday, and you're just feeling dizzy now. Tell them you were off because you hurt your knee. You were about to come back, but then this head thing happened. Okay? Don't ruin this trade by telling them when you got the concussion. I'm warning you. You don't want to mess with me. Keep your mouth shut, and I leave you alone. You kill the trade, and I'll destroy you."

"Hockey's a business," Rocket said dryly.

"That's right. And if the Giants get wind that you were already hurt, they can veto the trade. I'm guessing you don't want that, either?"

"I would agree with that," Rocket said.

"Then be smart and keep quiet. The story is you never told us anything. You thought it would go away. They'll scream and yell, but they can't prove it if we stick to the story. You'll be a Giant — and we'll have the player we want. Deal?" Floyd held his hand out.

Rocket reluctantly shook it. It made him sick to his stomach to touch Floyd's hand, but this wasn't the time to make a scene.

"Coordinate with Kirk and Nadav about getting your equipment shipped over and all that stuff. I have no idea how it works." Floyd offered a shrug. "Well . . . good luck."

He spun on his heel and headed to the stairs.

Rocket closed his eyes, let his shoulders slump and took a few breaths to let it sink in.

New beginnings or the end of the line? The Giants were one of the worst teams in the league.

And what if they refused the trade because of the concussion? Would they believe him? He had to make them.

The fans were streaming out the exits. He pushed against the wall.

"It's Rockwood!" Crawford said, waving a Racers foam finger in the air. His friends were right behind him.

"Hey, guys. Tough game," Rocket said.

"We got to get you back on the ice, bro," Chaz said.

"That'll have to wait a while," Rocket said.

"The injury still bugging ya?" Crawford said.

"It is, but it's not that. I've been traded. To the Tennison Giants. Me, Strauss and Rogers for a guy named Steve Bannister."

Their smiles faded.

"Brutal, bro," Chaz said.

Griff slowly wrapped his scarf around his neck. Rino pouted.

"Well, we wish you good luck," Crawford said. "Hope the injury clears up soon."

"Thanks, guys. You're truly awesome fans," Rocket said. He shook each of their hands.

They left a sombre group, which suddenly made Rocket feel sad.

A trade! That meant he wouldn't see Rory — or Ritchie and his family. It would be a painful goodbye, especially to Rafa and Leona. He'd really grown attached to them.

He set off to the dressing room. Barker and Floyd could take a hike. He wasn't leaving without saying goodbye to the boys — and Kaufman and Nadav.

Nadav stood outside the door. "Rocket, I just heard. They made the deal during the game, in the third period."

"Blywood told me hockey's a business, so that makes it all good," Rocket joked.

Nadav thumbed at the door. "Let me see if it's okay for you to go in. Barker's giving the boys his *opinion* about the game."

Rocket could hear Barker shouting.

"Apparently, he's not happy," Nadav said.

As Nadav opened the door to go in, Rocket could hear Barker ranting. "You guys better get it through your thick skulls that . . ."

A minute later, Nadav came back out, his face ashen. "He's going to be awhile. And he said you should just go. Straussy's already gone, and they pulled Rogers out of the game. He just left, too."

Rocket shook Nadav's hand. "You're too good a guy to be working for them."

Nadav shrugged. "Trainer jobs with a pro team are hard to find. I need the experience."

"You and me both," Rocket said with a laugh.

"Where are *you* going?" Rocket heard Barker yell as the door opened again.

Rory and C.C. came out.

"Wanted to say goodbye," C.C. said. "You'll do good with the Giants. I know it. I like your game."

He and Rocket shook hands.

"Brutal," Rory said. "Nothing wrong with a fresh start, though. We'll talk."

"Thanks. And say goodbye to Melissa and Angela."

"Will do." Rory gave Rocket a bear hug. "A trade is nothing, part of the game. Keep focused and you'll make it."

"Not sure it's worth it," Rocket said.

The door opened again.

"This is ridiculous!" Floyd said.

The rest of the guys were coming out.

Rocket shook all their hands.

"We get traded around, we fight, we get cut, but in the end we're hockey players first and foremost," Goldsy said. "Coaches, owners, GMs, they forget that."

"I'm sorry I didn't get a chance to play here too long," Rocket said. "I have tons of respect for you guys, and it was an honour to play with some real pros. Good luck the rest of the way. I'll see you when Tennison plays Pinewood in the finals."

"Least you can do is let us win," C.C. joked.

"I hear the Giants are getting this awesome new centre, so I doubt it," Rocket said.

"Okay, boys," C.C. said. "Let's get back in there. We need to absorb more hockey wisdom."

They filed back in, their faces stern. Rocket could see Barker and Floyd standing in the middle of the room. He wasn't going to miss them.

"Did you guys enjoy your little vacation?" Floyd said. "Am I the only one who gets that we lost tonight?"

The door closed.

"Take care of yourself," Nadav said to Rocket. "Give that head time to heal. Don't let them intimidate you into coming back too soon."

"I just hope they let me stay," Rocket said. "Anyway, thanks for all your help, Nadav. I bet we'll meet again."

"You'll get me box seats when you're in the NHL," Nadav said.

"You won't need them. You'll be an NHL trainer by then."

"Sounds like a plan," Nadav said warmly, and they shook hands again.

As he walked to the lobby, Rocket pulled out his phone and texted his mom and Maddy about the trade.

Maddy texted back almost immediately. *Sorry. At least it's a new start?*

André must have been with her because he sent a text, too: *Got rid of Barker. Huge move. Go Giants!*

Rocket texted Megan next.

She sent back ten crying emojis and added, *Don't give up. You'll do great on the new team. Giants can totally crush racers — seems like a good trade.* ☺

His mom's text came next. *Sorry, honey. Hopefully it will be a better team for you. Call me when you get to Tennison. Luv u.*

He put his phone in his pocket. All of them expected him to report to the Giants, same with all the guys on the team and the management.

Rocket was less sure. So many conflicting thoughts ran through his head.

He was worried about his injury, but he was also tired of moving and leaving everyone behind. And he was tired of being treated like a piece of meat — he'd been cut and traded so many times, and no one seemed to care what he wanted.

But then again, he didn't want to give up. He'd worked so hard and sacrificed so much. And the people he loved most in the world didn't want him to quit, either. So maybe he wasn't being selfish by giving it one more try.

That's when he made a promise to himself. This was it. First, he had to get healthy — completely. Second, he was going to register for some courses immediately. Third, he had to become a starter for the Tennison Giants and get on their top line by next season — and if that didn't happen, then he'd pull the plug and get on with his life.

If his mom and Maddy needed him to work, he'd do that. If he could go to university first, all the better.

At last, plan B was set. There would be no going back on it.

CHAPTER 29

Leona wiped her eyes.

"I'll see you again soon," Rocket told her. "And I'll definitely remember your birthday. It's in November, right?"

"It's in April!" she shrieked. "You're such a forgetter head."

"I'll remember now," Rocket said, laughing. "I promise." He gave her a hug.

"Do you have your lunch?" Mariana said.

"I have it. Thanks again for breakfast. I still feel bad about you guys waking up so early."

"Don't forget your sticks," Rafa said, holding them up.

"I won't."

"Call us when you get to Tennison," Ritchie said.

"I will."

"And remember the sandwich — and I put an apple in your bag, too," Mariana said.

"Okay."

"Don't forget my birthday," Leona said.

"Never!"

Rocket hugged Ritchie and Mariana. "I can't thank you enough," he said. "It would've been awful living here by myself. I won't forget how you welcomed me in and took care of me. And I'll still pay rent until you get a new person to take my room."

"Stop that," Ritchie said.

"No, I'm paying. Just like I promised," Rocket said. He ruffled Rafa's hair. "These brats are expensive."

"I won't take it," Ritchie said.

"You will," Rocket said.

They both burst out laughing and hugged again.

The passengers began to get on the bus.

Strauss had gone ahead with his wife and Rogers. With all their luggage and equipment, there was no room in the car for Rocket. He'd said he was fine to take the bus.

"Let's get Bryan's things on," Ritchie said.

Rafa rolled Rocket's hockey bag to the baggage compartment underneath the bus. Leona pulled his suitcase over.

"You be careful with your head injury," Ritchie said. "Very crazy to play too soon."

"I need to play, and I need the money," Rocket said.

Ritchie looked sad. "We do many crazy things for money."

Mariana had tears in her eyes. "Call your mother when you get to Tennison. She'll be worried."

Rafa and Leona grabbed Rocket by the waist.

"We don't want you to go," Rafa said. He wiped his eyes.

Rocket crouched and reached into his pocket. "You don't deserve these, because you beat me in crazy eights all the time, but here you go. Something to remember me by." He gave them each a big lollipop.

Their tears disappeared.

"Thanks!" they said, throwing their arms around his neck.

"Let Bryan on the bus. He has hockey to play," Ritchie said.

"Send me a Giants sweater and a hat," Rafa said.

"Hush, Rafa," Mariana said.

"Me, too," Leona said.

"Take care of your parents for me," Rocket said to the kids as he stepped onto the bus. He found himself with tears in his eyes. He really couldn't have lasted in Pinewood without them. He offered a final wave and went in, taking a window seat in the back.

A neatly dressed older woman sat next to him. She had grey hair and kind brown eyes.

"Where are you off to this morning, dear?" she said.

"I'm going to Tennison."

"Visiting family?"

He didn't feel like having a long conversation. "I have friends there."

"That's nice," she said. "I like Tennison, it's a pretty town. Where are you staying?"

Rocket's jaw tightened. He'd forgotten to book a hotel. He really was a forgetter head. "I, um, have a room . . . with my friends."

He let his head fall back and closed his eyes. He just needed a half-hour nap. Then he'd search for a hotel and start scoping out places to live.

The lady next to him shook his arm gently. "Did you say you were going to Tennison?"

Rocket opened his eyes. "Yes. Sorry, I zonked out there for a bit."

"I'd say. You slept the entire trip."

Rocket sat bolt upright, his heart pounding. He looked around wildly. "We're here?"

"I believe so."

He looked out the window. They were at a bus station.

"Excuse me," he said to the lady.

She stepped out to give him room.

"Have fun with your friends," she said.

"What friends?"

She looked puzzled. "The friends you're visiting."

He remembered. "Oh, yeah — sorry. Still waking up. I will. Thanks."

He grabbed his backpack and went to the front.

"Is the compartment open?" Rocket asked the driver.

Her mouth dropped open. "Are you kidding? We're leaving."

"I have to get off," Rocket said. "This is Tennison, right?"

"I called three times," the driver said.

"I think I was sleeping."

The driver groaned, pushed a button to open the door and then stomped off.

Rocket followed sheepishly. He pulled his stuff out of the compartment. Then the driver shut the door and lumbered back. Moments later, the bus pulled away.

He took out his phone and texted his mom and Ritchie: *Pulled into Tennison. All good. Off to the hotel. I'll call later.*

Then he googled *budget hotels in Tennison.*

"Excuse me," a young woman said. She was tall, athletic looking, with long brown hair tied neatly in a ponytail. She looked serious, but friendly.

Rocket moved aside.

"Actually," she began. "I was just wondering—"

"Sorry, I don't live here," Rocket said, figuring she was looking for directions. "I don't even know where I'm staying tonight."

"Well, if you're Bryan Rockwood, then I think I can help with that."

Rocket stared at her in surprise.

She held out her hand. "I'm Kati Rodriguez, the Giants' GM."

"Really?" he said.

"It's true," she said, wryly. "Women can be professional general managers, too."

"I didn't mean that." Rocket shook her hand. "I just didn't expect anyone to meet me."

"I sent Kirk Blywood about ten texts, but he never responded. So I spoke to your teammate, Turner Rogers, and he told me you were coming on the bus. There aren't many from Pinewood, so I figured this had to be it. Anyway, let's go."

"I can take a taxi."

"I have a van. Don't be silly."

"You don't have to. Besides, I haven't found a hotel yet. I fell asleep on the bus and didn't book anything."

She was trying not to laugh, which unnerved him. What was so funny?

"I'm hoping to find shared accommodations," he went on. "I stayed with this great family in Pinewood, and that worked out pretty good. It's less money, too. I'll get on that tomorrow."

Rodriguez smiled. "We've taken care of all that. I'll go over the rent and things when you're settled in a bit. I'm sure you're eager to unpack. I hope you don't mind sharing a room. It's a house with four guys, plus you, of course. Turner is there already. Strauss has a place with his wife and daughter."

She grabbed his hockey bag and sticks.

"I can take that," he said.

"Not the first hockey bag I've had to carry. I played eight years in the CWHL — the Canadian Women's Hockey League — and on three Olympic teams." She gestured toward a parking lot. "Come on. I'm over there."

He grabbed his suitcase and followed her across the street.

"I understand you had a bit of a problem — a missed meeting?" She opened the back of a van.

He froze for a moment. "Yeah. It was . . . complicated. And I got suspended."

"I noticed you haven't played for a while. I guess you're coming off an injury?"

"I was . . . But, unfortunately, I just got dinged up in a practice. It might be a concussion."

She put his hockey bag down and rested her hands on the butt ends of his sticks. "You have a concussion? When did that happen?"

"A few days ago. I didn't tell anyone. Sorry. I thought it would go away. Didn't seem like a big deal at the time — and then I started feeling a bit . . . sick."

She gave him a close look. "Can you work out?"

"Um, a little bit."

Rodriguez shook her head slowly. "This is so typical of Pinewood. They're such weasels. Floyd thinks he can make a fool of me because I'm a woman? Guess again. I'm going to the league commissioner on this. I should've been told."

"He didn't know," Rocket lied.

"Nothing personal, but I didn't agree to trade our best player for a guy with a concussion. I asked for full disclosure. They said you'd been hurt, but you were fine now."

Rocket shrugged helplessly.

She threw his stuff in the van. "May as well go to the house. I'll have to sort this out. Not sure where that leaves you. Probably back in Pinewood."

He couldn't let that happen.

"I don't actually know if it's a concussion," Rocket said quickly. "I just feel a bit . . . off. If I could have another week or two to rest up and work out, I'm sure I'll be fine."

"Rest up for two weeks? We need you to play, though frankly, we weren't exactly trading for you. We wanted Turner Rogers. We knew Floyd had it in for him — something about Rogers dating his daughter. We kept going over different combinations, and you ended up getting tossed into the deal."

Rocket took a moment to absorb the news.

"Nothing personal," she said. "Rogers is a big kid; he's over 215 pounds and is six foot three. And he's mobile, with good hands."

"He was on the fourth line with me," Rocket said.

"All I can say is, leave it with me. Come to the office

tomorrow, at the arena, around eleven o'clock, and we'll talk. It'll give me time to consider my options."

"Ms. Rodriguez?"

"Yes?"

"Please, don't send me back. Once I heal, I'll be one of your top players."

He knew he sounded pathetic. But if they sent him back, he would quit. This was it. He didn't have it in him to put up with Barker and Floyd. Especially after this deal fell through.

Rodriguez pointed to the van. "Let's just go to the house."

Fifteen minutes later, they pulled up in front of a two-storey house with a large gable in front. The porch was a bit crooked, and the windows looked old. The house was painted white, but flecks had fallen off, revealing blue paint underneath.

They hadn't spoken once during the entire trip.

"Do you know what the rent is?" Rocket said, as she opened her door. "I know I might not stay, but—"

"We'll go over that later," she said.

"Because I won't be paying rent?" he said.

"I don't know yet," she said simply. "Let's get you settled. They're nice guys, and you know Turner already, of course."

Rocket made sure he got to the trunk first and pulled out his hockey bag and suitcase. He wanted to show Rodriguez he wasn't that messed up.

"Let me take something," she said.

"I got it." Rocket wheeled the bags to the porch steps, slung the hockey-bag strap over one shoulder and hauled it and the suitcase up.

He waited for his head to begin aching.

He was tired, but his head felt clear.

A good sign?

He'd given up being positive. The best he could do was hold on and wait for tomorrow.

CHAPTER 30

The car pulled over in front of the arena.

"Thanks for the lift, Straussy," Rocket said. "I'll catch up with you guys later."

"No worries. Good luck in there," Strauss said.

"Be cool, bro," Rogers called out from the back seat. "Stick to the story."

Rocket waved as they drove off. Strauss had come over last night, and with Turner they'd talked late into the night about what Rocket should do.

They had a lot riding on this, too. If the trade was cancelled, it might be back to Pinewood for all three of them, and nobody wanted that. The Giants probably represented Rocket's last shot at the NHL, and Strauss and Turner felt this was a second chance to restart their careers. Strauss told them that Floyd had also threatened his career if he said anything about his hamstring.

The lies were piling up.

The rink wasn't nearly as fancy as the Pinewood Barns. It was a bit shabby, actually. Rocket liked old-school rinks, though. He could feel the thousands of games that had been played here. The dusty smell was comforting — it reminded him of where he'd played house league. That rink had a wood ceiling and a concrete floor in the lobby, with the classic concession stand off to the side. He used to bug his mom for french fries after every game, and every once in a while she'd buy them.

The fries had actually been gross — bland and soggy — but at the time he'd thought they were the most delicious things in the world. They were such a rare treat, and somehow they'd helped ease the sting of his father never coming to see him play.

Hockey might be a business to Blywood and Floyd and Rodriguez, but it had been the joy of his life back then. Like Goldsy said, they were hockey players first and foremost. The money was important, but not more important than the game and not more important than his honour.

He stopped in front of a door marked *Tennison Giants, Office,* and he paused.

He thought about Ritchie.

Ritchie cared about his family and worked hard. He was honest and kind. And he'd stood up to Carl because that was the right thing to do. That was who Rocket wanted to be: someone people respected. And someone who could respect himself.

He knocked on the office door.

"Come in," a woman said in a loud, gruff voice.

He opened the door and went in.

The woman had her feet up on a desk, and her hands behind her head. She wore a Giants sweater and a pair of faded blue jeans. Her hair was cut short, and she had large, round black-rimmed glasses.

"I'm Meredith Kasich," she said. Her tone made it clear she assumed he knew her name.

"Nice to meet you."

"You've met our general manager, Kati Rodriguez," Kasich said. "This is our coach, Violet Jackson. They both played together on the Olympic team. Now, you may think it's a bit odd to have women running a men's hockey team. People thought it was odd when I started an online travel website fifteen years ago, too, and odder still when I had an all-women board of directors." She shrugged. "No one freaks out if everyone in management is a man, do they?" Rocket could tell she had given this speech before.

"Um, no, Ms. Kasich," he said.

"And when I sold that company for three billion dollars and bought this team, everyone freaked out again. A woman can't own a hockey team — impossible!" She threw her hands over her head and laughed. "Just wait to see what they say when I buy an NHL team."

She put her feet down. "I was born in Tennison," she continued. "I live mostly in New York and Los Angeles now, but I still consider this my true home — always will. I used to come to this rink with my dad when I was a kid, even before I could walk.

"I love hockey, and I want to turn this franchise around," she said. "We're going to do it the right way and build it from the ground up. That means solid drafting, good coaching and a focus on player development." She nodded at Coach Jackson.

"Rodriguez told us that you have a concussion. Is that right?" the coach said.

"That's right. I . . ." He gathered himself. He wasn't going to start the rest of his life as a liar. He felt bad for Strauss and Rogers, and he hoped this didn't wreck their trade. But he also knew he didn't want to be a snake like Raymond Floyd. It was time to set things right. "I need to apologize to you, Ms. Rodriguez. I didn't exactly tell the truth. I got the concussion over a month ago."

"Did the Racers know?" Jackson said.

"Yes."

"Did Floyd know?" Rodriguez said.

"He did."

Kasich sat back in her chair, while Jackson shook her head slowly.

Rodriguez slapped her hand on the table. "Floyd is such a slimeball. I'm calling the commissioner. I'm getting this trade reversed, and I'm getting Floyd fined."

Rocket felt a chill run down his spine. "I understand why you're mad. I'd be mad, too, if I were you. But I also know Straussy and Turner are totally psyched to be here, so I'm hoping you can keep them."

"Why did you lie to us?" Kasich said.

"I was thinking about that last night. It's a little complicated. It goes back to why I got traded. Straussy had hurt his hamstring, and—"

"I was told he just tweaked his hamstring," Rodriguez groaned. "This is getting better and better."

"Hold on, Rodriguez. Give him a chance to explain," Kasich said. "Go on, Bryan."

"He doesn't think it's serious," Rocket said. "I'm sure he'll be okay. Anyway, like I said, Strauss tweaked his hamstring in a warm-up, and Floyd and Coach

Barker ordered me to play in his place. I said no, because I still have a concussion. Floyd freaked out and told me I was suspended again. He traded me that night to you guys. After he told me about the trade, he said I had to lie about the concussion or he'd make sure my hockey career was over."

Rocket took a deep breath. He was determined to tell the truth — all of it. "I know I'm not the biggest guy in the world. Everyone's been telling me I'm too small to play hockey since . . . maybe since I started playing hockey. But I outwork everyone, and I never quit. I love the game too much. And I've been lucky, I guess, to get this far. I've sacrificed a lot and so has my mom.

"I've been dreaming about playing pro hockey for so long it's a part of me. I almost can't imagine doing anything else. It was the hardest thing in the world for me to refuse to play. I had the feeling my hockey career was on the line if I said no. But if I'd taken another hit, I could have been permanently injured. I didn't want my family to have to take care of me for the rest of my life, just so I could prove I'm tough.

"I'm not going back to the Racers — I won't play for Floyd or Barker. If that means I'm out of hockey, then I guess it's time for me to find a job and help my family that way. You'll do what you have to. I totally get that. But I'm finished lying, and I'm done with the Racers thinking they control me."

Rodriguez's arms were crossed. She looked over at Jackson. The coach remained perfectly still, pokerfaced.

Kasich had a big smile on her face. "What do you think, ladies?"

"He's scrappy, I'll give him that," Jackson said. "I

also checked out his stats from junior. The kid can score — and you guys keep telling me we have trouble putting the puck in the net."

"He's also a kid with a serious concussion. He hasn't played in over a month. And then there's Strauss's hamstring," Rodriguez said. She rolled her neck. "Floyd is laughing at us."

"There's something else," Rocket said. "This is actually my second concussion, though Barker doesn't believe me. I got cross-checked in one of our first games of the season, and then I got hit in the head a few days later. That's why I was suspended. They didn't want to have to pay me for a week."

"Bryan, I appreciate your honesty," Jackson said. "I can see you're a thoughtful young man. But you have to understand the situation we're in. We need to get good, young talent and to start winning games. We're not only in last place, we also have the lowest attendance in the league. We have to get better — fast. How do we know you'll ever play again?"

"You don't," Rocket said.

"Let's give Ray-Ray a call," Kasich said. "Bryan, can you wait a moment?"

Rodriguez called out the number, and Kasich dialed it on the desk phone.

"Hello?" Floyd answered.

"Hello, Raymond. It's Meredith. How are you? Behaving yourself?"

"As always, Meredith. I assume you're not."

"Never have. Never will." She laughed deeply. "I wanted to thank you for Bryan Rockwood."

"Oh. Well, I think it was a good trade for both teams."

"Definitely. Definitely. A delightful young lad. First class." Kasich leaned closer to the phone. "The only problem is it seems he's injured, and quite seriously. A concussion. Did you know anything about that?"

The line went quiet.

"Am I on speakerphone?" Floyd said.

"I'm with Rodriguez and Jackson," Kasich said.

"Hello, ladies," Floyd said. "I'm here with our coach and general manager, also."

"Hi," Barker and Blywood chimed in.

"Right. So, about the concussion?" Rodriguez said.

"A concussion? Are you sure?" Blywood said.

"I think so. Bryan told us himself. Said he got hurt a while ago," Rodriguez said.

"That's impossible. We certainly didn't know," Floyd said.

"I'm not saying you did," Kasich said. "It's just that we know he didn't play for over a month, and he says he got a concussion over month ago, his second, I believe. Isn't that odd?"

The phone went quiet again.

"What are you suggesting, Meredith?" Floyd said, finally.

"I'm suggesting the commissioner might find this *oddness* very interesting. The commissioner might actually think you traded an injured player and didn't tell us. And let's not get into Strauss's hamstring issue."

"I don't know anything about that," Floyd said.

"Should I call the commissioner right now and ask him what he thinks?" Kasich folded her arms, leaned back in her chair and put her feet back up on the desk.

Even though it seemed like his hockey career was

over, Rocket was enjoying listening to this. It was good to have Floyd in the hot seat for once.

Floyd cleared his throat. "Okay. So, I'm assuming you want to reverse the trade. How about I sweeten the deal instead?"

"Keep talking," Rodriguez said.

"I'll send you another guy—" Floyd began.

"You aren't getting Colbert or C.C. or Goldsy. No chance," Barker said.

Rodriguez put her hand on Kasich's shoulder.

"How about you toss Brett Downey into the trade?" Rodriguez said. "He played with that Rogers kid, didn't he? I think you said they were wingers on the same line. That would make sense. We could keep them together."

Rodriguez looked over at Jackson. She flashed a thumbs-up.

"That's four guys for Bannister," Barker said. "C'mon."

"Should I conference in the commissioner?" Kasich said.

Someone groaned on the line. Rocket thought it sounded like Barker.

"Fine," Floyd said. "Whatever. We'll see who's laughing when we win the championship this year."

"I'll email you the trade sheet," Rodriguez said.

"Sounds good," Blywood said.

"Hey, Meredith — it's Coach Barker again. Let me give you some free advice. Get rid of that punk Rockwood. He's an undersized, arrogant goal suck, who has about as much chance of making the NHL as the chair you're sitting in. The guy is a cancer in the dressing room, and he's allergic to his own end. Dump him."

"Thanks for your honesty, Coach Barker," Rodriguez said. "We'll think about it."

"You should," Barker said.

"Boys, I believe our business is concluded," Kasich said. "Raymond, I almost forgot to ask, how is my dear Stella? I assume she's as beautiful as ever. Still singing?"

"She doesn't have a lot of time for that these days," Floyd said. "She's fine."

"Good to hear," Kasich said, her smile almost too big for her face. "Take care, boys."

She hung up and burst out laughing. "Stella sings like a frog with laryngitis, and those boys are as dumb as hammers." She slapped the table and shook Rodriguez's hand. "It's the art of the deal, Bryan. Never show your cards at the table, and move in for the kill when you sense weakness. Floyd is a pale imitation of his father. He has no guts. I knew he'd fold like a cheap suit and throw in another guy to make this go away."

"You're amazing," Rodriguez said. "We got four young players for Steve Bannister. Steve's a good player, but he'll never make the NHL."

Kasich pursed her lips and narrowed her eyes. "I like you, Mr. Rockwood," she said to him, "and I've learned to put my trust in people with character. It took courage to come in here and tell the truth. Floyd's a bully in the true sense of the word, and I have no doubt he threatened all sorts of terrible things if you told us the truth. You take your time and get better, and then show us what kind of player you are. Besides, if Barker hates you, I bet you're amazing. He sounds like a bigger dummy than Floyd."

She began to laugh again, and Jackson and Rodriguez joined her.

This was his second chance. He'd stick to the promise he made himself. Tonight he'd sign up for courses. Then he had to get healthy and make the first line — and he had two seasons to do that.

Feeling more optimistic than he had since being sent to the Racers, Rocket joined in the laughter.

CHAPTER 31

The first thing he noticed was the sharp sting of the cold air in his lungs. Next were the sounds: the scrape and click of his blades cutting into the ice, the echoes of his teammates calling to each other. He heard pucks booming off the boards or thudding dully as they bounced off a goalie's pads. Finally, he felt the wind in his face as he whirled behind the net and up the boards toward centre.

He'd sat out another two months. It felt more like a lifetime. He'd watched hour upon hour of video, taking notes and reviewing them. And he'd worked out endlessly, both in the gym and on the ice. He'd done hundreds of skating and shooting drills on his own — always on his own.

And then, as suddenly as the concussion symptoms had started, they'd disappeared. One morning he woke up and felt completely himself again. The doctors advised him to wait two more weeks to be sure, and that was the hardest time of all. But now he'd finally been cleared. This was his first practice.

He snagged a puck in the corner, cruised behind the

net and began stickhandling rapidly. He'd done this a million times in his life, but it had never felt so sweet. There was a moment when he'd thought — when he'd believed — that hockey was over for him. This felt like a new beginning — a gift.

Concussions would always be a worry, so he'd been given a special helmet with added protection. But the doctors said he'd made a full recovery. They'd also said that he may not have had a concussion after all. It might have been a soft-tissue neck injury, probably from the cross-check and made worse by Carl. That type of injury often had the same symptoms as a concussion.

Rocket could only hope that was true. He wouldn't take hockey for granted, in any event.

Tweet! Jackson gave her whistle a blast. "Give me the first power-play unit at centre. I want to work on the man advantage for the first half of the practice." She looked around and finally settled on Rocket. Pointing her stick at him, she said, "Bryan, why don't you and Turner be the forwards for the kill. Don't let them gain the zone too easily. We want them to have to dump the puck in. In our zone, maximum pressure on the puck at all times. Don't give the power play time to set up. Okay?"

"Sure, Coach," Rocket said. He would have agreed to anything she said, as long as he was on the ice.

He had watched every practice and game. He'd become a big fan of Rogers, and they'd become good friends, too. Rogers's confidence had been destroyed by the Racers, and for the first month here, he'd been tentative. But recently he'd begun to use all his skills, especially his speed. The result was four goals in the past six games. Downey had been playing better, also — and so had Straussy, once his hamstring healed.

"Let's see if I can do it," Jackson said. The goalie at the far end moved aside. She stickhandled the puck a few times and then fired it down the ice. The puck flew up in the air.

The guys let out a huge roar. She'd hit the crossbar.

"A good omen, boys," Jackson said, laughing.

The puck had bounced over the net and into a corner. The five players on the power play raced back to set up.

"I'll pressure," Rocket told Rogers.

He needed to skate. Too much pent-up energy.

Rocket slowed at the blue line. Rory and he had gone over this a million times. There were basically three strategies when pressuring the puck on a penalty kill. When the puck was deep in the attacking team's end, you could settle in front of their net and force it up one side; you could chase and make them pass the puck quickly, hopefully forcing a bad pass; or you could hover in the high slot, like a neutral-zone trap, and wait for them to bring it out.

He opted for number two. They wouldn't be warmed up yet — and he was too hyper to wait.

Rocket put it in high gear and charged into the left corner. The defenceman saw him coming and fired the puck behind the net to his partner. He did it a bit too early, which allowed Rocket to veer to the right before he went too deep. The puck jumped over the defenceman's stick, and he had to reach back for it. Rocket lowered his right shoulder and drove him into the boards — not too hard, he was a teammate — but hard enough to prevent the pass. The defenceman kept the puck in his skates, and he kicked it back along the wall. His defence partner grabbed it and set up in behind the net.

This time, Rocket settled in the slot, a metre or so to the left. He'd force the puck up the right side toward Rogers. The centre curled behind the net and set off up the right side. The defenceman took the bait and passed it to him. Rocket anticipated and left a bit early. He extended his stick with his right hand to take away the easy pass inside.

The centre backhanded it off the wall to the trailing defenceman. Rocket had already put on the brakes. He poked at the puck, and the defenceman had to retreat. Rocket drifted to the high slot. The defenceman sent it cross-ice to his defence partner, who redirected it to his right winger, hovering around centre.

The penalty-killing defenceman pinched, and all the winger could do was knife it off the wall and down the ice. Rocket thought it might be icing, but Jackson didn't call it. It was only practice, after all. He back-checked hard and had reached his blue line by the time his defenceman had collected the puck.

For a second, Rocket contemplated a quick break up-ice for a long stretch pass.

That was definitely old-Rocket thinking.

He was killing a penalty. A twenty-metre pass up the middle of the ice, when they had an easy chance to ice the puck, was plain dumb.

Rogers had taken the top zone to the right. Rocket decided to support his defenceman by setting up in the high slot instead. It proved a good decision: the defenceman slipped him the puck to avoid a forechecker. Rocket slid it to Rogers, who calmly slapped it down the ice.

Tweet!

"Okay, this isn't going all that well," Jackson said. "Forwards, you're not moving your feet, and that leaves the defencemen stranded with the puck. One guy is basically shutting you down. You have to be moving all the time, curling to present yourself for a pass, and then you attack as a unit once you gain the neutral zone." Jackson leaned on her stick. "Let's switch the power play up. Give me Rogers on right wing and Downey on left. And Bryan, you take centre." Jackson pointed at two other players. "You take over the penalty kill up front."

She took the puck on her stick. "I won't try it again. I'm not feeling it." She shot the puck the length of the ice, into the left corner. It caromed behind the net, and the goalie trapped it for his defenceman.

Rocket had spent so much time thinking about defence, it was weird to switch gears and focus on scoring. He felt good, though. He'd shown off a bit of his new defensive skills. Hopefully Jackson had noticed.

The defenceman held the puck. Rocket curled behind the net, and the defenceman shovelled the puck forward. Rocket had to take it up the ice himself.

He continued up the right side. Rogers was at the far blue line. Downey was cutting across the ice, from left to right. The forechecker was a bit slow coming across. Rocket didn't hesitate. He pushed hard and evaded the forechecker's outstretched stick. Then he cut left to put space between himself and Downey. Rogers headed across the blue line to the left side.

Rocket crossed the red line. He glanced back ever so slightly and noticed his left defenceman close behind. Rocket dropped the puck and kept going. Just as he hit the blue line, the puck was dumped into the left corner — perfect timing. Rocket got there first. He snapped a pass behind the net to Downey, who trapped it at the half-boards on the right.

The opposing defenceman followed through with a hit — a real hit — on Rocket, but Rocket was ready and it didn't hurt. Most important, his head and his neck didn't hurt. It felt good, actually, like he was finally playing again.

Downey gave it to his right defenceman and went down low to the right of the net. Rogers set up in front. Rocket took Downey's spot by the boards. The puck slid across the blue line and ended up on Rocket's stick. He gave it to the point, who passed it right back.

"Make something happen, Power Play," Jackson yelled. "Move around."

Rocket brought the puck close to his left foot with the tip of his blade, ducked his left shoulder and then exploded to his right, flicking the puck over the stick of the penalty killer. He felt a slash on the back of his leg as he cut into the high slot. It hurt, but he didn't care. They had an overload, basically four against three.

Rogers established himself in front of the goalie. The goalie crouched low and peered around him from the left. Rocket had a lot of choices: a short pass to the defenceman on the right side, a pass down low to Downey on the same side, or a shot himself.

He angled his body sideways, puck on his forehand, faked a shot, faked a pass to the defenceman and then saucered a pass to Downey. The goalie dropped to his butterfly and slid toward Downey. Downey surprised Rocket by saucering the puck right back. It was a perfectly placed pass about two metres from the goal line.

Rocket had played too much hockey to even have to think about what to do next. With Rogers still screening the goalie, Rocket snapped a wicked wrister to the top corner. The goalie flung out his blocker. Too late.

The players on the bench banged the boards with their sticks, and Jackson blew her whistle.

"That was nice. Good puck movement," Jackson said. "All five guys touched the puck — quick passes and active feet. Turner, good net presence. Love it. We need guys paying the price. Bryan, nice shot."

Tweet!

"Give me the puck," she said to the goalie.

He dug the puck out of his net.

"I feel lucky," she said. "I'm going to have a run at it!" The goalie at the far end slapped his stick on the ice and moved aside. Jackson pulled the puck back and let it fly. The puck flew high in the air — and landed about three metres in front of the net. The goalie slid over and saved it with his pads.

Jackson slapped the ice with her stick. "That sucked. I wasn't focused." She looked up. "Power-play unit, I just iced the puck. You guys want to set up?"

Rocket laughed. Then he slapped his wingers' pads and took off.

He was ready for the next play.

CHAPTER 32

"Go, Giants, go! Go, Giants, go!"

The crowd had been cheering and clapping to the beat of the organ since the warm-up. Rocket was a bit surprised, considering the team's record.

"They're a bit crazed tonight," Rocket said to Rogers, as they cruised across the red line.

"It's free pizza slice night," Rogers said.

"Let's pretend they love us," Rocket said, laughing.

"Bring it, boys!" Downey yelled. He slapped his stick on the ice and set off on a mad dash around the rink.

Rocket and Rogers let out a cheer. Rocket had already done a few laps, but he was still so energized, he felt ready to blast off into outer space.

The siren sounded, and Rocket coasted to the bench. The crowd rose to its feet, and the national anthem started. Rocket couldn't stop hopping from foot to foot, like his feet were on fire. It felt like forever since he'd played.

"How long have you been dancing professionally?" Rogers asked him.

"I'm too nervous. It's been so long, it feels like I've never played before," Rocket said.

"Well, that's the blue line," Downey said. "I'll explain the red line later. I don't want to confuse you."

"This is our chance," Rocket said. "Coach Jackson thinks we're three kids. We've got to show her we're only here for a quick visit. We're heading to the big club."

"I like your thinking," Downey said. He whacked Rocket's shin pads with his stick.

The play was fairly wide open at first. Jackson was on them to calm down and take better care with the puck. Their goalie had to bail them out a few times. Rocket was happy with his first three shifts. He'd had a shot on goal, and for the most part, the play had been in the offensive zone. He took a sip of water. The ref whistled the play dead in the Giants' end.

"Rockwood's line out," Jackson ordered.

Rocket hopped over the boards. Faceoff was to the goalie's right. The opposing centre, number 12, was already there. Rocket had read up on him. He'd been in the league a long time.

"So they're sending in the young guns," number 12 said. "Isn't this a little late for you? It must be bedtime."

"Maybe it's time for you to retire already, old man. You're never going to make the NHL now," Rocket quipped.

The centre grunted. "Everyone's got a big mouth. You've been in the league how long? Like an hour? No respect for the game."

Rocket knew he'd gone too far. He hadn't shown

the guy the respect he deserved. "Not true," he said quickly, tapping the centre's shin pads. "Much respect here. Have a good one."

He hunched over the dot.

"Hard one, Rocket," Rogers said.

Rocket nodded ever so slightly. That was their signal for a faceoff play.

The puck dropped. Rocket chipped it to the right. Rogers cut inside the circle and took it in full stride. Rocket slipped past the centre, brushing against his left shoulder, and took a short backhand pass. The opposing defencemen backed up furiously to keep the play in front of them.

Rocket took the puck across the blue line and fed Downey cross-ice, and then Downey one-timed it to Rogers on the right side.

They were on a three-on-two.

Barker had always been on Rocket about taking unnecessary chances to try to score. Rocket's time away from the game, which he'd spent learning everything he could about defence, had taught him the truth — a great player also knows when to take a risk. He'd learned that at this level, when it was time to go for it, you gave it everything you had.

Rogers cut inside. Rocket crossed behind him. He didn't even look. He knew Rogers would deliver. A metre from the blue line, the puck was on his stick. He pushed to the outside. The left defenceman held his stick out to angle Rocket into the boards. Rocket accelerated, then leapt into the air as the defenceman threw a hip check. He caught a piece of Rocket's leg. Rocket bounced into the boards, but the impact didn't knock him down. He landed on both skates, stumbled slightly and regained his balance. The puck was in his feet. He kicked it to his stick.

"Rocket!" Rogers yelled.

Rocket backhanded a pass to Rogers at the top of the circle. The left defenceman veered over to pressure the puck. Downey stormed into the zone from the left wing, although he was being checked closely by the right winger. Rogers waited for the left defenceman to commit to him, and then he slid a pass back to Rocket near the faceoff dot to the goalie's left. The shot was open — but Rocket had a better idea. The winger covering Downey kept coming into the zone. Downey had cleverly slowed up and was open. Rocket waited to freeze the goalie and then he rifled a pass across the zone to Downey, who one-timed a slapper on goal.

Ping!

The puck nicked the crossbar and deflected into the netting.

"Brutal," Rocket groaned.

Rocket went to the faceoff dot to set up. Number 12 looked mad, probably irritated at himself for letting a rookie make him look bad. Rocket didn't kid himself. This next faceoff would be tough to win outright. Number 12 was a real pro, and he'd been doing this a long time.

"Be sharp," Rocket said, calling the play.

Downey bounced his stick on the ice. He got it: Rocket would try to tie the centre up. Then Downey would come across and steal the puck.

"The young guns are hungry for goals," number 12 said.

The young guns. Rocket liked it. "We're just here to win, same as you," he said.

"Good luck," the centre said. He almost seemed to mean it.

Then the puck dropped. And Rocket and the young guns brought it.

EPILOGUE

The camera lights flashed. Rocket had to turn away and blink a few times.

"What do you think will be the key to winning?" a voice called out.

Rocket wasn't sure which reporter had asked the question. There were too many of them, and the lights made it hard to see their faces.

"We have to play our game and not get caught up in the hype," he said.

"Aren't you nervous? How do you deal with the pressure?" the reporter pressed him.

"That's not easy," Rocket admitted. "Ever since I was a little kid, I've dreamed of being here, of being in this situation. I guess every kid who's ever laced up a pair of hockey skates has had the same dream. I'm lucky enough to live it. I think about that, and the nerves go away."

"But you've had bad luck, too. You didn't have it easy getting here. Weren't you cut from your minor bantam team?" another reporter said.

The reporters laughed.

"The coach said I was too small — and maybe I am," Rocket said to further laughter.

"No, really," the reporter said, and she came closer. Rocket suddenly recognized her. It was Rita Martin, the same reporter who'd interviewed him at his first NHL training camp. Hard to believe that was five years ago.

"You were a low draft pick in junior," Martin said. "The last round, in fact, and you were a low pick in the NHL draft. You were sent to the Pinewood Racers in the AHL, then traded after a few games to the Tennison Giants. Five years later, you're in the Stanley Cup finals — against the same team that traded you, no less — on one of the best lines in hockey. It must seem like a miracle now. But back then, did you ever think of quitting?"

He let his mind wander back.

"There were times when I thought, 'Rocket, this isn't going to happen.' When the Racers traded me, I was battling a neck injury. My future was uncertain, and I was close to quitting the game and getting a job. My family needed the money. But then I lucked out with the Giants. They gave me a chance, and it paid off for both of us."

"Is that your message to kids — never quit?" Martin said.

"I'd say it's important to have a dream," Rocket said. "But it's also important to have lots of dreams. And you have to be prepared to work for them. I said it was luck that got me here, but it also took a lot of hard work and sacrifice. Sometimes, you need to take a step back and ask yourself if it's worth it, and the answer will be different for everyone."

"You grew up without much money," Martin said. "I've heard that you've used some of your salary to buy your mom a new house and pay for your sister's med school. Was that also a dream of yours?"

"Absolutely. They've supported me and my dream for so long; it's been great to help them out." He'd also convinced Ritchie and Mariana to accept a loan. They were both going back to school so they could get better jobs.

"And you've paid for your own education," Martin stated.

"That's right. I've been taking online university courses for a while now. I should have my degree in another year or so. I think my mom cares more about that than hockey — or the house."

That got a chuckle from the reporters.

"I came to realize that getting an education was like having a plan B," Rocket went on. "I guess that's my message to kids: don't put all your eggs in the hockey basket. If you get injured, or don't make it for whatever reason, an education gives you options." He thought of Rory. His knee had blown out again, and that was it. He'd had a really hard time for a while, but now he was an assistant coach in the AHL.

"So, do you think the Young Guns are ready for this?" a reporter called out from the back.

Rogers, Downey and Rocket had quickly made the first line on the Giants, and they'd been kept together in the big club. Somehow that nickname had followed them to the NHL.

"We're a bit nicked up, for sure," Rocket said. "It's a long season, plus we had the three playoff rounds to make the finals. But the guys in the other room have played just as much, so we have no excuses on that front. We're excited, yeah, but we don't feel like we've accomplished anything yet. That will happen when we hoist the Stanley Cup."

"Why do you think you made it when so many others didn't?" Martin said. She certainly asked tough questions.

He had to think about that. "I used to believe it was all about desire; that you have to want it more than the next guy. It took me a long time to realize that while effort is a big part of it, luck and timing are also huge factors. I've had a few bad coaches, and I was cut a few times. But then I had some really great coaches, too. They took chance on me despite my size, and I learned a lot from them. I've also only had one serious injury, and I was lucky that it healed as well as it did."

Rodriguez came onto the podium. "Okay, guys, I think that's enough Rocket time. He needs to get ready."

Rocket stepped away from the table. "Thanks, everyone."

"Rocket, just one more question," Martin called out. "You and Turner Rogers finished first and second in league scoring, and Downey finished in the top fifteen. Can the Young Guns be stopped?"

Rocket turned back to the table.

"We don't think like that. We're a team, not a line, and we win and lose as a team. If we don't score, then we make sure we play great defence and wait for someone else to step up. That's how it's been all season. Our team has a saying—"

"Bring it!" the reporters chorused.

Rocket laughed. That saying had gotten around — like their nickname.

"Right," he said. "That means you play hockey the right way: unselfish, hard, fast and smart. It's not about our line scoring. It's about our team winning."

He waved to the reporters and left the stage.

"Coach will take questions after the game . . ." Rodriguez said.

Rocket walked down the hall, back to the dressing room. He felt good about his answers. Too many boys sacrificed their childhoods for the NHL dream, and maybe he'd done that also.

He hadn't been completely honest about one thing, though. He was totally nervous about tonight. The first game of the Stanley Cup finals — his heart had been beating a mile a minute since he woke up. He pulled out his phone and sent his wife a text: *Miss you. Speak after the game.*

Megan texted back: *Focus!*

He walked into the dressing room. The boys were hanging out. A few were blowtorching their sticks or applying tape, others were talking in groups of twos and threes — the usual hockey stuff. Their hockey bags sat on the floor in front of each stall, and above them, stuck to the upper shelves that ran around the room, were their name tags.

On the far wall, between *Turner* and *Brett*, he saw it: *Rocket*.

Luck, hard work. Whatever it was, it was still kind of cool when a dream came true.

Bryan "Rocket" Rockwood is faced with the unthinkable: being cut from the Huskies — the AAA hockey team he has played on for three years. With no other teams interested in him, Bryan reluctantly joins a AA team, the Blues, at his best friend Maddy's insistence.

Things only get worse when Rocket sees that the Blues don't take hockey seriously. Facing the Huskies in the round robin will give Rocket the chance to prove his skills, but to keep his hockey dreams — and his friends — Rocket must realize that while hockey is his passion, it is not his entire life.

★ Winner, Rocky Mountain Book Award
★ Nominee, Silver Birch Award

ISBN 978-1-4431-3375-3

LAST SHOT

David Skuy

The exciting sequel to *Rocket Blues*!

The OHL — it's the next step on Bryan "Rocket" Rockwood's path to a pro career and a better life for his family, and he can't wait for training camp. But as the smallest guy on the ice, it will be tough enough for Rocket to make the team, even without worrying about hazing from the other guys. He has the skills and the drive, but will that be enough to earn his teammates' respect and a spot on the final roster? Or will he finally have to give up his hockey dreams?

★ Nominee, Manitoba Young Readers' Choice Award

ISBN 978-1-4431-4669-2